The Flight of Andy Burns

THE

FLIGHT

OF

ANDY BURNS

Stories

ALICE

MATTISON

William Morrow and Company, Inc.

New York

Some of these stories have appeared in the following magazines: "The Hawk on the Fence" in *Grand Street*, "The Library Card" in *The Mississippi Review*, "Strawberries" in *The New England Review*, "The Flight of Andy Burns" and "A Winding Stair" in *The New Yorker*, "The Landlord" in *The North American Review*, "The Crossword Puzzle" in *Shenandoah*, and "Whom Did You Kill?" in *West*.

It is the policy of William Morrow and Company, Inc., and its imprints and affiliates, recognizing the importance of preserving what has been written, to print the books we publish on acid-free paper, and we exert our best efforts to that end.

Library of Congress Cataloging-in-Publication Data

Mattison, Alice.
    The flight of Andy Burns / stories by Alice Mattison.
        p.   cm.
    ISBN 0-688-11118-1
    I. Title.
    PS3563.A8598F55   1993
    813'.54—dc20   92-21641
                                                            CIP

Printed in the United States of America

First Edition

1 2 3 4 5 6 7 8 9 10

BOOK DESIGN BY CYNTHIA KRUPAT

For Savita, the other side
of the first conversation

CONTENTS

The Flight of Andy Burns

THE

LIBRARY

CARD

Shelley and Robert's older daughter, Johanna, is five, and she has just learned to write her last name. Now she may have her own library card. On a Saturday afternoon, Shelley and Robert and Johanna and the baby, Lily, go downtown to the library.

The children's librarian is shelving books when they come in. "Spooks," she calls to them. She doesn't mean anything bad, she means that just now she is interested in ghosts, though it's not October. Shelley and Robert and Johanna and Lily (who is asleep in the Snugli on Shelley's chest) must wait while she leafs through a book to find the most delicate, most peculiar illustration. "I haven't thought about this book in years," she says. "It fell into my hand. It was a favorite of my sister's."

The book is dense with fat paragraphs. Shelley

doesn't think Johanna would like it, or, really, that *she* would, and she'd have to read it aloud. She busies her hands with Lily and at last the librarian puts the book down. All celebration and flourishes, she takes an application for a library card from her desk. Johanna promises to take care of the books she borrows, and then she settles down to write her name while her father, who taught her to do it, watches but does not allow himself to comment. Johanna's name has many letters—she has Robert's last name, Horowitz—and she writes each of them large. Her name doesn't fit in the allotted space and she must write the *t* and the *z* in the margin below.

"It's a good thing we didn't give her a hyphenated name," says Shelley, whose last name is Simpson.

"When I was eight," says the librarian, "the girl with the longest name in my school was Constance Mastropietro. Constance is a surprisingly long name for only two syllables."

Johanna gazes at her and hands over the form. The librarian looks at it and says that they must now go upstairs to the adult library, where the woman at the desk will type up Johanna's library card.

"Come on, Mommy," Johanna says. "Bring Lily."

They all climb the stairs and wait while a middle-aged Hispanic woman finishes typing something. Then she takes Johanna's application. "It's illegible," she says abruptly. "She can't have a card."

"But the children's librarian approved it," says Shelley, who is confused. It is true that Johanna's signature is illegible. Of course it is illegible.

"Sorry," says the woman. She turns back to her type-writer.

Shelley doesn't know what to do. She is filled with an astonishing rage, which she can feel in her hands and arms and shoulders as if something palpable has been injected into her body. "Wait a minute," she says. "Wait a minute." She would like the woman—who is ignoring her—to die, and she would have sworn a moment ago that nothing this woman could do would make Shelley want her to *die*.

"Will you please listen to me?" says Shelley, in a voice so loud and angry that there is a shocked hush for a moment in the main room of the library, where people are consulting the card catalog, checking out books, and talking quietly.

The woman turns. "Ma'am, I'm going to have to ask you to leave the library if you insist on making a scene."

"Will you listen to me?" says Shelley, only slightly more quietly. "My daughter has been practicing all week. This *matters*."

"I'm sorry," says the woman.

"Don't you *want* children to read library books?" Shelley is shouting. She is angry at everyone she can think of except Johanna and Lily, whom she clutches as if she thinks the Snugli might fall off. She is angry with Robert, who is standing at an angle that could mean he is just someone waiting to speak to the library worker. Shelley moves a hand in his direction as if to turn him.

Lily gives her first waking-up cry, and Robert speaks.

"This lady shouldn't have to decide about Johanna's card," he says smoothly. "Is there someone else we can ask?"

"My supervisor is in there," the woman says, and points to the reference room, where a young black woman is sitting behind a desk.

"Thank you," says Robert. He takes the application and

goes into the reference room. Shelley moves a little away from the desk. She sees Robert explaining, and then the librarian in the reference room laughs. "Sure," Shelley hears her say. She takes the application from Robert and then returns it to him.

He comes back to the desk, not smiling but looking eager, as if he is the sort of person who is always willing to follow elaborate directions if he can just be sure he will be praised for it. He is not that sort of person at all.

"She initialed it," he says cheerfully to the library worker, pointing to the corner of the application.

"Well, all right," says the woman. She types a library card and hands it to Robert, who hands it to Johanna. Then they all go back to the children's room, though Lily is whimpering by now. Johanna says she will select books quickly. Robert follows her to the shelves and Shelley seeks out the librarian.

"She wouldn't type the card up at first," she says. Her voice shakes.

"Really? I should have taken it up myself."

"She said it was illegible."

"*I* could read it perfectly," says the children's librarian. "And I have terrible trouble with handwriting. I could *never* be a mailman."

When Johanna has chosen four books and the librarian has stamped them out, they leave the library. Shelley is still angry but she can see around the edges of her anger. She could push past it, or she could enter it and have a fight with Robert. They cross the green toward the mall. It is winter, and the green is windy and bare. There is old snow here and there. It is a raw, cloudy day—Shelley hopes for new snow. Lily is crying quietly. Johanna has handed her books to her father and is chasing pigeons across the green. She is wearing a red jacket with a hood, and she has red boots on and a red plaid skirt, pleated, like one Shelley remembers wearing as a child. Around her neck is a blue-and-white muffler that was knitted for her by Robert's mother.

"Well, that worked out," says Robert, and Shelley's hand moves quickly to Lily's back.

"I hated what I did. I hated what *you* did," she says.

"What was wrong with it?"

She cannot explain. "First you just *stood* there."

"I was letting you do your bit," he says.

"You think I *wanted* to yell like that?" she says. "And then you manipulated her."

Now he is angry, too. "I gave her a way out. People who act like that, you have to give them a way out."

"Don't you see how conniving that is? And it made it worse that she was Puerto Rican."

"Racial tolerance requires that I scream at her?"

They have reached Chapel Street, and Robert takes Johanna's hand—she has come running to catch up with them. They cross together. "Look," he says to Shelley, "it doesn't matter that you lost your temper."

"That's not what you really think," she says. She is teary, and Lily is crying now—she wants to be nursed. They go into the mall and up the escalator, and then they come to the food court, where there are tables and chairs and take-out food shops lining the walls. The windows look out across Chapel Street at the green—over near them, it is almost like being outdoors.

Shelley takes both children and chooses a table. She finds a tissue in her pocket and blows her nose. Robert goes to buy food. He will bring chocolate milk and a cookie for Johanna, tea for Shelley, and coffee for himself. Shelley takes Lily out of the Snugli and then the baby starts to cry hard. She takes the Snugli off and opens her coat. She pushes her chair back from the table and shrugs her coat off as well as she can, shifting Lily, in her pink nylon bunting, from one arm to the other. She pulls her sweater up a little and puts Lily in position to nurse. Lily's mouth fastens immediately on Shelley's nipple and Shelley feels the release and relief of her sucking.

"They had the tea you like." Robert has forgotten they were having a fight. One of the shops carries tea bags, but not always Shelley's favorite, cinnamon.

Lily turns her head at the sound of Robert's voice, letting go of the nipple. Shelley coaxes her back to the breast. Lily turns again to find Robert, but then goes back to sucking, while Shelley dangles the tea bag in the hot water with her free hand. Johanna is talking about the people she can see waiting for the bus on Chapel Street below them—a woman with twins in a stroller, another woman who looks something like her kindergarten teacher. Robert sits down and takes the lid off his Styrofoam cup of coffee.

Shelley is thirsty. The tea will be good. She slips her free hand in between herself and Lily to unzip the bunting a little, and then she eases the hood off Lily's head. She strokes Lily's smooth dark head and feels the pulse under the soft spot move as Lily sucks industriously.

Then Robert says, "I wish that didn't bother me, but it does."

"What bothers you?"

"Breast-feeding in public."

Shelley looks around. There aren't many people in the place at this time of day. "Nobody cares," she says lightly.

Suddenly his voice is low and urgent. "Shelley, when I came along, she was turning her head in every direction, and your entire breast was exposed."

"Oh, it wasn't. That was just for a second—"

"How do you think it looks—"

"Nursing—" she begins. But she has forgotten her anger. It comes back. "If you cared about your baby—"

"Stop it," he says. "I said it was something I couldn't help feeling, I didn't—"

She doesn't want to listen or, this time, to cry. Now she wants to overwhelm him with argument.

"Daddy." Johanna is shaking his arm. "Daddy, read me this book." She has finished her milk and cookie and has been looking at the library books. He looks annoyed, but he does begin reading aloud in a low voice. The book is *Lyle the Crocodile.*

"Listen to me!" Shelley says. She waits restlessly, ripping pieces off her empty Styrofoam cup while Lily nurses on the other side, and then she straightens her sweater, being careful not to expose her breast—but surely she is always careful—and burps the baby on her shoulder.

"We have to go," she says, finally. Robert is reading the last page of the book.

"Mommy, my scarf!" says Johanna. "I lost it."

"You must have been sitting on it." Shelley is distracted from her anger and they look for the muffler amid the tangle of their coats. It is gone. "Did it come off when you ran after the pigeons?" she says.

They all stare hard out the window and across the green,

and Robert says he can see something blue and white. It
is just starting to get dark outside. "Wait here," he says.
"I'll go get it."

It doesn't make sense for Shelley and the children to
wait, because their car is parked near the library and they
will all have to cross the green anyway. But before she can
say anything Robert has sped away from them.

"Can I go too?" Johanna says, but Shelley says no.
Johanna is restless, but after a short time they can see
Robert at the corner. He crosses Chapel Street. It doesn't
seem to have occurred to him that his family can see him,
and he doesn't turn to look, but Johanna and Shelley watch
his progress, fascinated, as if he were on television or in
a movie. Shelley notices the way Robert walks—he moves
his arms and keeps his head down. He's wearing a navy-
blue watch cap. Does he keep his head down because he's
looking for the scarf, she wonders, or does he always do
that?

Then Shelley notices that someone walking on the path
is waving at Robert, and she sees that it is their friend the
children's librarian, who has finished work and is crossing
the green in the twilight on her way home. The librarian
waves and waves, but Robert, heading off to the right, not
walking on the path, doesn't see her, and as Shelley
watches him go farther away and her come closer (but at
Chapel Street the librarian turns away from the mall and
disappears), she imagines how Robert might see the librarian and forget Johanna's scarf, now invisible to Shelley
in the twilight (though Shelley never actually *saw* it), and
run toward the woman, who thinks he is a kind man, the
sort of man who'd go look for his child's scarf when it's
lost, not the sort who'd rush off without sense when if he'd

just stayed and helped her get the children organized they could all cross the green together. Shelley could take both children and meet him coming back—there is no real reason to sit here—but it is as if she cannot, and now she pulls her anger around her like a dark quilt. She rests in her anger at Robert, who is ashamed that she nurses Lily in public, and in her mind she sends him at an angle from his path and straight into the arms of the children's librarian, who rises up on her booted toes and skitters to meet and embrace him.

That is Robert, then, a trivial man who is probably having an affair with the librarian, a man who thinks breasts are secrets.

But Robert has reached the scarf and now he picks it up—it *is* the scarf—and in the deepening darkness they can just see him wave it in the air, signal with it and even dance with it for their benefit. He has realized that they'd be watching, and though he is ashamed of her honest working breasts he isn't afraid to make a fool of himself dancing alone on the green, which makes Shelley so angry that her anger falls over the top—the top of what?—into whatever is on the other side, a kind of tiredness with laughter in it. She laughs at Robert. He must have been a wreck in the library: embarrassed, of course, when she yelled, and thinking he shouldn't be.

"Can you put on your coat?" she says to Johanna. She often manages alone with both children, and she knows how to lay Lily on the table and then stand blocking her in case she chooses this moment to learn to roll over, while she puts on her own coat and buttons it. She ties Lily's hood and zips her into the Snugli again and then she can help Johanna with *her* hood. She puts the library books under her arm and takes Johanna's hand and they all go down the escalator and outside. It's snowing. It seems less cold than it was before, as if the snow in the air could keep away the cold. Shelley crosses Chapel Street with her children and starts across the green. Robert has seen them and is almost there, running, holding up the scarf in case they have somehow managed to miss seeing it so far. Snowflakes touch Shelley's face, soft ones. It was a terrible mistake to marry Robert, for he is not perfect, and she will have to pound him with her words and tears so many more times before she fixes him, so many hundreds of times.

THE

LANDLORD

I was following the Sabbath prayers at my cousin
Marion's synagogue, flipping pages forward and
back, reading the English (I don't know Hebrew),
when the descriptions of God's power and maj-
esty—and *importance*—began to seem alarm-
ingly close to what I think about my lover, Jerry,
when he's getting to me. I thought it would be
hard to feel as wrought up about God as I do about
Jerry, although Jerry is not powerful and majestic
at all—he isn't even the human equivalent. He's
a Libra. Jerry's boyish (his hair is light and
straight and falls in spikes toward his glasses, he
has freckles) though he's not a boy; he has two
daughters in college. I have a son, Adam, who's
fifteen. Jerry's marriage, like mine, ended a long
time ago.

Sunlight was coming through the windows of
the synagogue in straight lines broken up by the

soft, thick shapes of people. There were a few old men in prayer shawls, who seemed out of place to me in this suburban temple. The sun looked warm, but wasn't. It was supposed to be spring, and I'd worn a suit because I don't have a decent spring coat to wear over a dress. The suit is bright blue and I like it. I thought that with my one dressy blouse (white silk with a ruffly neck) it would be right for Corky's bar mitzvah, but I froze on my way in from the parking lot, and during the service I was still cold. My feet felt funny in heels, too, after nothing but boots for months. In fact, outside there were still patches of ice here and there.

Marion is Corky's mother. I wouldn't miss her boy's bar mitzvah, although I hadn't been in a synagogue for a long time and my own son didn't have a bar mitzvah and wasn't even present for Corky's—he was visiting my ex-husband.

I tried to think whether God *could* be more important to me than Jerry, whether I was doing something seriously wrong that I could do differently. I had hoped that Jerry would come with me to Corky's bar mitzvah, but I didn't ask. I just mentioned it and waited to see what would happen, so I wouldn't actually be refused. This was not brave.

There was a telephone booth in the lobby, I remembered—I thought I remembered—and if I went outside, walking quietly, letting people think I just needed to go to the ladies' room, I could call Jerry to say hello and hurry back. No, not to say hello: to tell him I was going to be braver in the future. Marion wouldn't think I was walking out on Corky—she'd just think I'd gotten my period.

I wasn't sure what sort of synagogue this was, whether members of the congregation would be offended if someone made a phone call on the Sabbath. They'd driven their cars on the Sabbath—the parking lot was crowded—but that might be different. The synagogue was only fifteen minutes from Jerry's house if I took the highway. Maybe ten minutes. What if I didn't make the phone call, but drove to his house. "I'm not angry, Claire," Marion would say to me later. Of course she'd be angry. "But I was terribly scared," she'd say. "When I saw you leave I assumed you went to the bathroom. Then after a while I thought you might be sick, and I sent Gail to look for you. Then I thought you were off having a nervous breakdown." Gail is her sister. Meanwhile, Jerry would tease me for ducking out of the bar mitzvah, and then we'd go to bed. I love the times he teases me, and I'd add what he said to my catalog of teases, to think about later. "You must have prayed efficiently to be done so soon," he'd say as we took off our clothes. I'd ask him to come back to the bar mitzvah with me, and we'd arrive in time for the second course at the buffet luncheon in the hall behind the sanctuary. Marion would get over being mad and an extra chair would be found.

I leaned forward to glance at my cousin—she was looking intelligent and reverent, wearing a challis dress in a subdued print—and I thought that I really might be about to climb over the old woman sitting next to me and scuttle up the aisle in my high heels, heading for the parking lot or the phone—or maybe just the ladies' room, after all, directed by the congregation, which I pictured turning around to watch me the way congregations turn around to watch a bride, with the gray-haired men who looked as if they'd been bused out from some dark *shul* on a twisted city street where sellers of kosher salami jostled yeshiva boys, sticking their arms out to send me the right way, disapproving.

But I stayed put, of course, and finally Corky went up to the altar. He was adorable. He *chanted* his Torah section, the old-fashioned way, and made his speech sweetly, looking at his parents and grandparents in the order he mentioned them with only a one-second delay. Later I had a moment with Marion—we'd all danced the hora and Mayim, which I didn't know I remembered, and my shoes and hers were lying in the same corner where we'd kicked them, so we had to sort them out and lean on each other to put them on, and we did a lot of back-patting, as if we'd taken a test or been in an audition.

"I was up all night," Marion said to me, and laughed.

"You don't look it," I said. "You look beautiful."

"You don't look it, either," said Marion. "No, that's not what I mean. I *mean*," she explained, more slowly, laughing again, "you look beautiful, too, Claire," which was an exaggeration, but even though my blouse was hanging out by that time, I knew that I did look nice.

·

Jerry is not only my lover but also my landlord. At least he isn't bigger than I am—we're both five-nine. When I wear heels I'm taller. Jerry and I met because of the house: I had to move, and I'd been living in an apartment, so when I saw a house advertised for rent, I was interested. It's not *exactly* the house he grew up in, but almost. His parents bought it when he was a senior in high school— as he once said to me, it's not the place he ran home to after the kindergarten teacher yelled at him, or the place where he gazed at the wallpaper next to his crib. His father and mother lived in it until eight or ten years ago, when they moved to Florida and started renting it out. Both of them died, one after the other, not long ago, and they left it to Jerry. When we started seeing each other I wondered whether he missed it and liked me just because I was *in* it, or whether he might be connecting me with his mother somehow, and it still feels strange when I turn from the stove or the sink—the very ones she used—and see him studying me, looking as if he's about to ask a question, except that he doesn't. At such times I'd give a lot to see with his eyes, but that wouldn't help; I'd just see a tall woman in bedroom slippers with walked-on backs carrying a steaming pot of spaghetti to the sink with two blue pot-holders and tipping it over quickly into the colander: a tangle of spaghetti flopping down, a rush of water, steam around my head.

We started going out the way you'd think. The first time I saw the house we had a long conversation, standing in the empty living room. Jerry conscientiously told me all the drawbacks of the house. "There aren't enough electrical outlets," he said. "The shower's not great." Then the day I signed the lease we had another talk, mostly about kids and jobs this time—he works for a union and I'm a nurse. The first time we had dinner together was the day I moved in. He stopped by to make sure everything was all right, and at last there were chairs to sit on, so we talked even longer. I found out his astrological sign. That might have been the first time he teased me, in fact. I work in a maternity unit, and when he told me he was a Libra, I said, "Baby Libras are OK," and then found myself explaining that once I had arranged to take my vacation in January so as to miss most of the newborn Capricorns.

"Capricorns are the hardest," I said. "You'd think Baby Tauruses would be hard, or Leos, but they're not, they're cute. Although an odd thing," I went on, thinking of something I'd noticed, "is that Taurus babies have Taurus mothers. Late April, most of May. I carry some baby in, and the mother's trying to get her nightgown off her shoulder and pull her breast out, and the baby is rooting around for the nipple and yelling, and then the mom looks up at me and says, 'Today's my birthday.' " Jerry listened to me seriously, there in my new and his old kitchen. He doesn't look as if he has *any* sense of humor; he looks as if he thinks slowly—but then he took out his car keys and offered to drive me to the medical library so I could write up my findings on this subject. For weeks afterward he'd suddenly come up with the name of another medical journal where, he said, I could publish my study.

We'd been seeing each other for a month or so by last Halloween. I liked Jerry but I wasn't in love with him yet. Adam was going to a Halloween party, being too big for trick-or-treating, but I was looking forward to handing out treats even on my own. In our old neighborhood few children had come by, but I'd heard that here there would be a crowd. So I made a jack-o'-lantern and bought those short thin pretzel sticks to give out (not too much sugar), and the night before Halloween I spent an hour putting handfuls of pretzel sticks into plastic sandwich bags and twisting the tops closed, hoping the local parents wouldn't mind that I'd handled the treats. I prepared forty bags. Meanwhile, Jerry called and asked me to have dinner with him the next night, and somehow I forgot it was Halloween we were talking about and said yes, and that he could pick me up at six.

When I got home from work the next day I didn't think about Jerry. I lit a flashlight in the pumpkin and put it on the windowsill and turned on the porch light. October had been warm, but it became cold right at the end, and the night was dry and crisp. Everything seemed to rattle, as if the leaves and grass had grown brittle all of a sudden. When the first children came to the door they were shivering in costumes made of cardboard or that stiff, thin gauze with faces printed on it, or clothes or bones, and there were parents hovering behind them with winter jackets to throw over their shoulders between houses. The next children were younger, and they had their jackets *on*, though open, and their witch and princess costumes underneath. They were holding out big paper bags for their treats. A minute later Jerry appeared, coming up the porch steps behind a pirate. He waited while the pirate got his pretzels. At first I wondered what he was doing there, then I remembered. "I forgot!" I said. "I forgot when we talked that it was Halloween."

Jerry looked upset. "You don't want to go out?" he said.

"Could we wait?" I did want to, though I'd *totally* forgotten—I'd been planning to scramble some eggs for myself. Jerry was wearing a coat and he took it off. He looked at the bowl of pretzels for a long time, as if it reminded him of something. "You got a little carried away, I think," he said, and took a bag of pretzels, untwisted the tie, and started eating them. "I love pretzels," he said. He broke each one in half before eating it. I don't know why. He stood there breaking pretzels and eating them and then when the doorbell rang he walked over quickly and opened it himself, the bowl of plastic bags under one arm—and was captivated by the two little kids, almost babies, on the porch. "Claire, *look*," he said urgently. He crouched to give them their bags of pretzels, very slowly and soberly, as I stood behind him watching, and then he closed the door and leaned on it, shaking his head and laughing. "Let's get married and have a baby," he said.

The children were wearing yellow sleepers with feet, and someone had sewn brown cloth strips to make tiger stripes on one of the sleepers. The other child was a lion with a long brown tail. Both of them were quite round— maybe they had their coats on *under* their sleepers.

I didn't say anything when Jerry said what he did—and immediately wished I had. The next person to ring the doorbell was a friend of mine with her own kids and her neighbor's kids—half a dozen altogether. Jerry opened the door again and Joyce, my friend, said, "Doesn't Claire live here?" and I stuck my head out and waved over everybody's heads, beginning to feel exhilarated.

"I'm Jerry," said Jerry. The next time I saw Joyce she said, "Is that guy living with you?"

"No."

"Oh," she said. "Usually you can tell if a person opening a door doesn't live there. He opened the door as if he lived there." I'd changed so much about Jerry, just since Halloween, that I got excited about what she said until I remembered that he once *did* live there—probably, I thought, that was all it was.

.

When Jerry collapsed against the front door on Halloween, laughing, it was as if something brittle snapped, freeing something sweet—but needy—in me that's still in me now. He has big teeth, and when he laughs they show, which makes me want to reach past them and touch his tongue. After Halloween one night, coming down the steps of a restaurant with an upstairs dining room, we kept knocking into each other and I felt, as he reached an arm out to me, safe in a way I've hardly ever felt safe. Once on the phone—"Are you there?" he said. "Are you there?" He'd left the phone for a moment to find something he wanted to read to me, something unimportant. I guess it was the tone of his voice that makes me remember it, as if he could hardly believe I'd still be there.

One Saturday I had to work—I've been at the same hospital for years and I can ordinarily get the schedule I want but this time I couldn't. I had told Adam to take the bus downtown and meet me when I got off, and we'd go out to a Chinese restaurant. Adam likes garlic chicken. I meant to bring a pair of pants to work so I could change, but I forgot, and so there I was with Adam, waiting to be seated in the Chinese restaurant in my white shoes and nurse's uniform with a sweater over it, when Jerry came along. He was surprised to see us even though he and I had been there together and had talked about how we'd both eaten in that restaurant for years and liked the same dishes. He'd come for take-out, he said. "Some of that shrimp all to yourself?" I said, but he didn't seem to remember our lengthy discussion of the ways this restaurant fixed shrimp. "I've been cleaning my apartment," he said.

"Why don't you stay and eat with us?" I suggested. "You can order your own shrimp if you can't bear to share them."

"I don't mind sharing," he said gravely, and he joined us, though when we were seated he looked uncomfortable, and Adam was quiet, too, though they'd met a few times by then. I found myself buttoning my sweater as if to hide my uniform, and in fact Jerry said, "So you really are a nurse."

I tried to remember whether he'd seen me in it before. "Of course I am."

"I love it that you're a nurse," he said. I didn't know what he meant but I didn't believe him; it was as if he'd said, "Don't be a nurse!"

"I'm a tired nurse," I said. I tried to keep from talking about my troubles—it had been a hard week—but I couldn't help it. We'd had a baby in the unit with problems, but when I started to explain Jerry looked so worried that I stopped. "We've got a wonderful pair of twins now," I added quickly. People always like to hear about twins. "Big babies—huge for twins. Over seven pounds each. I've been hauling them around all day, one on each arm."

"Mom, can we have dumplings?" said Adam.

"Let's have an order of dumplings, OK?" I said to Jerry, but he just said, "Babies—I don't know how people start with babies. How does anyone have the nerve?" He picked up a fried noodle and put it back into the dish. "When Jemima was born—" he said. Then, "Jemima's my older daughter."

"I *know* who Jemima is," I said, suddenly upset. We'd discussed both his daughters in detail. "She's thinking of changing her major. She broke up with her boyfriend. Her roommate is from Brazil."

"I'm sorry. I didn't remember I told you."

We had the chicken and the shrimp and we ate with chopsticks. I loved the shrimp—I always do—and I kept talking about how good they were, and how good it was that we'd met there, trying to convince myself. When the fortune cookies came, Adam's said, "You are lucky in

love," which made him blush and crumple it up. I knew
he was starting to think about girls last fall, but he couldn't
admit it yet. I kept thinking Jerry or I might have reached
for that cookie. I usually have a feeling about which cookie
is mine, and in fact Jerry had taken that one. Mine shat-
tered when I opened it. My fortune said, "You will hear
bright words," which I loved, of course. I put the strip of
paper in my pocket and ate the cookie bit by bit, picking
up each piece with a dampened fingertip. Jerry broke his
cookie open carefully, so it came apart into just two pieces,
but it had no fortune inside at all, and he pushed it away—
and that's how he was most of the winter, in just that mood.
At first I thought it was something particular—something
I'd done or something that had happened to him—but
slowly I realized that he wasn't going to blurt anything out
to which I could say, "Oh, is *that* it?"

But some days were good. Bed was good. I treasured
his rare merriment as if it were a tiny animal curled nearly
out of reach, a bit of soft fur I could stroke with just one
finger.

·

When I got home from the bar mitzvah I brought the
mail in and put it on the dining room table. It was about
four o'clock in the afternoon. Jerry hadn't said anything
about dinner that night. Adam wasn't coming home until
Sunday, so I could not only have dinner with Jerry but
stay over at his place if he wanted me to. I wondered if
he remembered that Adam was away.

I went up to my bedroom and took off my shoes, which
was a relief, and put on my slippers. Then I went back
down to look at the mail. The dining room was dim so I

turned on the overhead light but it didn't work. I assumed the bulb was used up and took the mail into the kitchen, where the afternoon sun comes in. I was still cold, or cold again, so I plugged in the coffeemaker—there was coffee left over from breakfast. But it didn't get warm—I kept touching it and it was as cold as ever. I realized the electricity was off, or at least a fuse had blown, which also explained why I was so cold—the thermostat is electric. I went through the house snapping on light switches. The lamp in my bedroom worked, though the one in Adam's didn't. The television worked. The bathroom light worked. I went down to the basement to look things over (the basement light didn't work). In my old apartment there were circuit breakers, but here there were fuses, and I didn't know anything about them. I had to call Jerry, and having an unassailable reason to call him gave me such a sense of luxury that I felt better and ran upstairs first to change my clothes and warm up—I put on slacks and a turtleneck and a heavy sweater and socks, while looking forward to making that phone call.

"I know circuit breakers but not fuses," I said to him on the phone.

"Do you want me to tell you what to do?" he said.

"No, I'm afraid of electricity." I was disappointed that he didn't immediately seize on my problem as an excuse to see me. "All right," he said then. "Maybe there was something I should have done. We'll come over."

"Who's we?" I said.

"Oh. Jemima," he said. At least he didn't say, "My daughter." "She's on her spring break—a surprise."

"I'd love to meet her," I said.

Both daughters had been in town at Christmas, but Jerry

hadn't suggested we meet, which at the time seemed like proof that he wasn't serious about me, although later I decided I'd expected too much. Now we hung up and, waiting, I couldn't settle down and do anything. I tried to pick up a little—the house was a mess. I swept the kitchen floor, then I actually went and looked out the window for them. Then I watered the plants.

Jemima came in talking. "It's not the *whites* that are high in cholesterol, it's the *yolks*," she was saying. Jerry was behind her, motioning in all directions, signaling her to be quiet and signaling a distracted greeting to me at the same time.

"You said Claire's a nurse," Jemima continued. "She'd know." She started unbuttoning her coat in a vigorous way, as if she were next going to toss it aside, push up her shirtsleeves, and rub her hands together. She was short and a little fat, not like Jerry at all. "I'm Jemima," she went on. "You're Claire. Hi. Did you know Dad has a cholesterol problem? Did he even *tell* you?"

"Jemima, baby—" said Jerry. He turned to me. "I had my cholesterol tested. It's not one of the bad categories, it's just above all right."

"My grandfather died of a heart attack," said Jemima decisively. Then, in a new tone, "This was his house. It's strange for me to come here." She stopped taking off her coat—it was cold in there, anyway—and took herself on a little tour of the first floor, hands in pockets and face suddenly looking like Jerry's—young, fair, freckled, earnest. Jerry came to stand next to me and shrugged a little as if Jemima belonged to both of us.

"Now," he said, "what's wrong with the electricity?" but his daughter interrupted him. "When Dad said you took care of newborns, I got very interested," she said. "I'm writing a paper for psychology about babies. I've worked in a nursery school, but I don't know anything about newborns. I need to know whether they have individual personalities."

I opened my mouth. "You don't have to answer now," she went on. "Maybe I could call you some time and sort of interview you."

"Sure," I said. "Whatever you want. Of course they have personalities. Each one is different." Is that true? I thought.

"I suspected they did," said Jemima. I wondered whether I would tell her I didn't care for baby Capricorns. I wouldn't want her to get the wrong idea—maybe *she* was a Capricorn.

"Now," said Jerry again. I led him through the house, showing him where the electricity worked and where it didn't, and then we all went down to the dark basement—I couldn't find my flashlight. It's a cluttered, spidery basement, with two dusty little windows. The fuse box is high up on a wall, and Jerry had to stand on a pile of lumber to look into it. "I'm not sure how this works," he said. There were some extra fuses on top of the box and he looked them over. Then he peered at the ones in the fuse box. "I think this one is bad," he said. He took it out and then he took one of the others and stuck it into the opening where the bad fuse had been. Immediately there was a flash of light, then darkness, and at the same time a sharp pop. Jemima and I threw our arms around each other. Jerry jumped off the lumber and took several steps back but nothing else happened.

"I guess we should have figured out what made it blow

in the first place," he said after a minute. We began touring the house again. When we reached Adam's room, where the lights didn't work and the clock had stopped—around the time that morning that I'd been comparing Jerry and God, I noticed—Jemima went over to look at Adam's computer. I'm allergic to computers, but my ex-husband bought him this one, and Adam spends hours fiddling with it.

"I think the switch is in the *on* position," said Jemima. Her father was behind her, looking at the computer too, looking serious. I thought that soon I was going to make up my mind about him—that I could probably be a sort of grandmother to this girl's babies if I wanted, that after all it was probably up to me.

"Adam's been away for three days," I said.

"Would he have left the computer on?" said Jerry.

"It's possible," I said. "He forgets things."

Jerry bent down and unplugged the computer and the clock, and I unplugged the lamp for good measure.

"Do you think that did it?" I said.

"I guess so," said Jerry. We went back downstairs and then he said, "I'll just go back to the basement and try another fuse."

"Dad, no!" said Jemima and threw her arms around him. "You'll be electrocuted. There'll be another explosion. Call an electrician. It's not worth it."

"Do you know how long it would take to get an electrician on a Saturday night?" said Jerry. "Don't worry. I know what I'm doing."

He went back to the basement. "I can't stand this," said Jemima, who was moving restlessly from room to room, looking somewhat accusingly at my electrical appliances. "Let me just—" She unplugged the television.

"Are you down there?" I called to Jerry, after the sound of his footsteps stopped.

There was a pause. "I'm *down* here," he said.

"You're all right?" I said.

"I'm all *right*," he said. "I'm a little nervous."

"Jerry, I can do without heat!" I yelled. "If you don't think it's safe, *never mind!*"

There was another pause. Then Jerry's voice floated up the stairs again. "I think it's safe, I'm just scared." Jemima and I looked at each other.

"I'm standing here holding the fuse," called Jerry, "and soon I'm going to put it in."

Everything that came to my mind—sex jokes, of course—was actually fairly funny, but not to be spoken to the poor man's daughter. Still, I started to laugh and so did she, and then we both turned serious, because we really *were* scared for Jerry, and then we both got silly again. His voice sounded faint, brave but faint. "I'm almost ready!" he called now, and we laughed again, and then I pictured a door flying open, and Jemima coming in with babies in both arms—*her* babies, or babies from the hospital, or babies she was studying, or maybe even *my* babies—coming in and handing me babies, sometime in the future. Then, "Let there be light!" called Jerry, his voice slightly high with excitement, as the overhead light in the dining room went on, just a modest sixty-watt bulb, but still, it made a difference.

BODY

OF A

SNAKE

The soup kitchen isn't a good place to think, but sometimes I do a little thinking there—less when Matthew is asking me questions. His voice is slightly stilted. "Have you done any miracles recently?" he asks; then a moment later—disappointed—asks again. "So. You haven't done any miracles?"

It's a place for having an opinion and stating it quickly. When we serve sausages in tomato sauce over spaghetti, Carey's opinion is that the whole pan of sausages should be dumped into the sauce. Carey is tall, thin, and sexy, and his long arms flip the pan gracefully, spilling a few sausages because he's swaying or almost dancing. I protest: the bottom of the pan is filled with grease! Carey says there's hardly any grease, grease don't do no harm.

The other day Matthew said he'd been to a

carnival where he saw a woman whose body below the waist was a snake's.

"I think she might have been a phony," I said. He was standing at the side of the table, leaning forward a little stiffly, his pale hair in his eyes, talking to me across Carey. Carey was serving spaghetti, then passing each tray to me. I was trying to do sauce and sausages quickly because there was a long line of people.

"No, she was a snake. She had reptilian scales."

Just then, Edith, from the kitchen, brought out a pan of sausages and Carey dumped them all, with grease, into the sauce. I threatened to hit him.

"I love pain," he said, and slapped his own cheeks, one after the other.

Also, he was giving out far too much spaghetti to each person. "Won't we run out, Carey?" I said.

"Trust me."

Taylor, who was serving peas that day, thinks we should serve the sausages on the side, just keep them in the pan and spoon them out three at a time. This is easier. When the sausages are deep in the pot of sauce, it's hard to scoop them up with the ladle. They are the long, thin kind of sausage. Mostly I have to use the slotted spoon to get them and then change to the ladle for sauce.

Taylor is sensible. I like his face, which is pock-marked—the little depressions on his cheeks gentle him. Someone once said he's a thief, but I don't know if it's true. Taylor's method of serving sausages works if there are enough servers: one for spaghetti, one for sauce, one for sausages, one for vegetables, one for dessert.

My opinion is that it's all right to dump the sausages in if the grease is drained out first. Even though it's hard to hunt for sausages, they taste better if they've absorbed sauce. When I first began to come here, I didn't say what I thought, because I'm a volunteer. Now I argue. The next pan of sausages came out from the kitchen, and Matthew was no longer telling me about the snake lady, so I was able to stop Carey and drain the grease.

Matthew never eats sauce—he eats his spaghetti plain, as a child might, but he isn't a child. He can spell any word you come up with. I once heard him say he's autistic. I was surprised—I didn't know that autistic people knew they were autistic. One day when he'd bothered me about miracles for a long time, I asked him if he was being metaphorical, and he said, "Partly metaphorical."

The day Carey served too much spaghetti was the ninth of the month. At the very beginning of the month it's not as crowded, because people have just received their checks, or they have friends who have checks. Then around the sixth it's getting more crowded, and the air seems a little snappy. Everybody's cashed their checks and some have spent the money to get high or drunk or whatever they get. I can't help liking the feel of the place then— it's slightly jumpy, slightly funny, slightly out of kilter, slightly frightening. More so if it has snowed. I don't know why.

As they pass the table and receive a tray, people complain about the size of the portions—it's expected, it's all but *required*—but the tone of the complaints varies. Sometimes sorrowful: "You honestly think that's enough sausage for a grown man?"

We don't give out more when they complain—we'd only run out sooner. "Everybody gets three," I say.

At other times, angry, especially at the end of the month. Once, a woman said to me, "You'd give more if you were serving your family." She spoke gently, not angrily. She was black and I am white, but she looked like an aunt of mine—the lines across the forehead, the angle of the mouth. "And what are you doing here?" my actual aunt would add if it were she, and though my uncle would say firmly, "She is helping the poor," my aunt would look uncomfortable—uncertain—and I don't know who'd be right.

When we ran out, the day Carey gave too much spaghetti, he kept on serving and dancing until the basin was empty. "Spaghetti!" he sang out then, and somebody at the other end of the table relayed the message to the cook, Marjorie, who came storming in from the kitchen. The water wasn't even boiling yet. We'd given out too much. And there was still a long line.

"So this woman at the carnival," Matthew said in a low, insistent voice, still standing—or standing again—next to the table. "She talked to me and everything."

People were annoyed that they had to wait. Some said they'd take their sausages on bread, and we made up those trays. One man shouted at us. "Every time I come, I have to wait," he said. "You give trays to the staff—they don't even stand in line."

It's true. The kitchen staff just comes over to us and interrupts when they have time to eat, and we give them trays. Matthew counts as staff, though he doesn't do any work. Carey had served him a lot of spaghetti, even more than the other people, because he never takes sauce.

"He had enough for three people," said the man.

"I'm telling her about a woman with the body of a snake," Matthew said to him.

A long line—mostly men, some women, one or two children—had formed, reaching all the way to the back of the room and partway across.

"Snake," said a man behind the first man. "Snake," he said slowly. "I know a woman, she be just like a snake."

The man next to him, whose head was bowed as if he was not paying attention, his chin almost resting on his black jacket, nodded slowly.

"But I be the animal that kills snakes," said the first man.

"A mongoose," said the man with his head down.

"You are right, brother. I be the mongoose."

"No," said Matthew. "She was a woman above the waist, but she had no legs." The men ignored him. "Instead of legs, she had a snake's body. But she talked to me."

"That was nice," I said.

Edith came out of the kitchen. "Spaghetti will be ready in a minute and a half." People shook their heads, and some laughed. More came forward to take their sausages on bread. We spread two pieces of bread in the large section of each tray, put sausages and sauce on top, and then passed it on for peas and dessert. The dessert was pretty good that day: Entenmann's chocolate cake. We'd been given a big stack of boxes, and a woman named Marion, who is quiet, was cutting the cakes and serving them. She doesn't ordinarily like to serve dessert because we run out of what's good and people get angry, but this time there was plenty.

"So," said Matthew, "did you ever see anything like that, a woman with a snake's body, talking to people?"

"I think maybe she was wearing a costume," I said.

"Oh, no, she was a real snake."

We had to wait for a long time, but at last Taylor brought a basin of spaghetti from the kitchen, and just then another pan of sausages came out, too. Before I could stop Carey, he dumped the whole thing in the pot. Then he took a tray from the pile and we began serving again. He still gave out too much spaghetti, but it didn't matter as much. It was almost closing time.

"*Shit,*" said a man I hadn't seen before, coming along in the line, a broad man in a gray sweatshirt with the hood bunched around his neck. He had a harsh voice. "You make me wait and then you give me *shit!*"

"What's wrong with it?" said Carey.

"It's *burned,* that's what's wrong with it. I could see the burn on those sausages—the whole pan was burned."

"I don't think so," I said. I used the slotted spoon to find three sausages in the pot for the tray I was filling. There were dark spots on them, but they weren't charred.

"It's shit is all. Shit," said the man.

"Watch it," said Carey.

"Who're you telling to watch it?" the man said swiftly. "Who?" and Carey put down his tongs and began to step from behind the table, but Taylor, who had stopped serving peas—Edith was serving peas now—and had just brought more trays from the kitchen, stepped sideways to block him and said, "Take it easy."

The man grumbled, but he took his tray, refusing

cake, and sat down alone at a table in the back of the room.

Carey watched him. "He wants to make trouble," he said. "He's sitting there where nobody else is. If he wasn't there, we could *clean* that table. We'll *never* get out of here."

"Forget it," I said, but Carey crossed the room, his high rear end bouncing, his legs sinuous. There were three or four people at each table except for the one where the man was sitting. Now a man and a woman with a little boy got up and took their trays to the kitchen, and one table was empty.

We couldn't hear what Carey said. He gestured toward the serving cart coming his way. Marion was starting to clean up, taking napkins and cups from the empty table and putting them on the cart. Then she squeezed a rag out in a bucket of hot soapy water and began to wipe the table. The man said something to Carey and kept on eating. Marion, who is peaceful and moves slowly, spoke to Carey, and Carey argued with her, but now he gestured less quickly. He came back to the serving table. Taylor was serving spaghetti. The line was diminishing, then it was gone. One or two more people came in, and then it was time to carry the pans of food to the kitchen.

I brought the pot of sauce in, and then I took a rag from the drawer, fixed my own bucket of soapy water, and went back to the dining room. I began to clean the serving table. Tomato sauce makes stains—I had to scrub. When I was done, three tables were empty and Edith and Marion were cleaning them. Taylor was wiping the dark-blue metal chairs and stacking them upside down on top of the tables, two in each pile. The man with the gray sweatshirt was still eating. Nobody was at the table right near him, and I went to clean it.

I wiped the chairs, then turned each one upside down and put it on the table so the seat and the back formed a triangle with the tabletop. It's tricky to put a second chair in place on top of the first without knocking the first one off. Carey pushed past me and hurried to get the mop from the closet. He filled the bucket. It was too soon—Taylor had just begun sweeping, and at two tables people were eating.

"We are closed!" Carey called out, though that was not his job—it was the manager's job, but she was in the kitchen. "OK, everybody, time to go!" He left his mop, took Marion's bucket and rag, and started wiping the table where the man with the gray sweatshirt was sitting. "Time to go," said Carey. The man paid no attention.

"We will never get *out* of here!" Carey said, and he swiped at the table, didn't bother to wipe the chairs, and began seizing each one by a leg and swinging them upside down onto the table. He surrounded the man with over-turned dark-blue metal chairs in piles of two, their chrome legs bristling up and out.

I put away my rag and took the other broom, and I began sweeping the part of the floor Taylor hadn't reached. The floor is dark red, large, and sometimes when I sweep it, the bits of food and clutter become the world and I forget where I am. That day, it was hard to sweep because of the peas. It took me a long time.

"I'm still wondering how it could be," Matthew said.

I was startled when he spoke. He was standing behind me.

I straightened up and looked around. The man in the
gray sweatshirt was the last guest left in the dining room.
I was near his table, and I saw that he was still eating,
his tray surrounded by piled-up chairs. Nobody else was
in the dining room except Taylor, sweeping near the serving
table, and Carey, leaning insolently on his mop, watching
the man.

"How *what* could be?" I said to Matthew. "How a woman
could have the body of a snake? Are you still thinking
about that?"

"How she could talk to me," said Matthew patiently. "I
want to know how she could be so emotionally normal."

I almost laughed. It had taken him so long to get
through to me, and then, in a moment, he'd done it. But
Carey said something I didn't hear, and the man in the
sweatshirt stood up so abruptly, his shoulders big and
taut, that I forgot what we were saying. Just before we
were interrupted, I had known, for an instant, how it
would be to have a snake's body below my waist: how it
would coil heavily on the floor, with my torso sticking
up awkwardly, teetering, how the small of my back, just
above the scales, would ache, how I'd vainly row my
arms along the ground, trying to move faster, my hands
dirty and raw. I would not be emotionally normal. I would
be in a constant, helpless fury of impatience and frus-
tration.

Then the man in the gray sweatshirt interrupted. There
was a sharp sound as he slapped the table hard, shouting.
Matthew jumped sideways, his arm knocking against the

piled-up chairs, and four of them slid easily to the floor. In the immense clatter, the man in the sweatshirt turned as if Matthew had hit him, and his hand was moving toward his pocket, but then his body changed again—became lighter, looser. Marjorie had stepped in from the kitchen and Elizabeth, the manager, behind her, and now the man was picking up his tray and telling them he never hurt nobody, they should know that by now, he never made no trouble, and he carried his tray into the kitchen on his way outside to the street.

THE

GREAT

BLUE

HERON

My son, Terry, was turning somersaults in the water. His narrow back curved and gleamed like a seal's as it disappeared, and then his head emerged—always in the opposite direction from where I somehow expected to see it. When his face came up he was grinning, his eyes were closed, and his hair was sleeked to his face.

I was sitting on the end of the dock. It was late afternoon, and soon it would be too cold to swim, but there was still a little sun in the cove. Then I looked up and a gull was coming across the lake—except that it was suddenly huge, squared-off, gray-blue: not a gull. It had long angled legs and its wings were stretched straight, almost awkwardly, as if the Wright brothers had just attached them. Terry looked up just as the bird veered *toward* him—to my surprise—and down. Then it climbed swiftly and settled out of sight on the branch of a pine tree. Terry waded out, wrapped himself in a towel, and hurried along the narrow wooden dock to where I sat.

"It was a Great Blue Heron," he said. He was eleven. He'd been reading the bird book. "I saw the folded neck. Only herons fly with their necks folded."

I saw movement behind the branch at which I was staring.

"That was the most frightening moment of my life," said Terry.

But I was trying to explain where the bird was. "Do you see that bent pine?"

"That was the most frightening moment of my life," he said again. I turned toward him.

"Well, he was sizing you up, all right. Or she."

"Male and female herons look the same," said Terry. "I looked up—and there he was."

"Right above your head?"

"Just a little to the left." He said he'd go up to the cabin for his binoculars. When he was gone, there was silence.

"I told Shoogie we saw a Great Blue Heron but she didn't care," he said when he came back. Shoogie is his name for his grandmother—my ex-husband's mother, Nina, who had come along with us on this week-long vacation in Maine. The name Shoogie was Terry's baby attempt to say Sugar, which was actually what she called him. Nina and I are friends, though I have been divorced from her son, Mark, for several years.

Now Terry tried to point the binoculars at the correct pine branch, but he still couldn't see the bird. He untied the canoe that was next to the dock. "Maybe if I go out a little." We'd been at the cabin for only a few days, but

Terry looked natural in the canoe. After a few strokes, he stopped and looked up.

"Can you see him?" I said.

"Yes, I see him perfectly," he said in his high, serious voice. "He's definitely a Great Blue Heron."

"I want to see. Come get me."

But the bird suddenly reappeared above the pine branch and grandly, complexly flapped away from us, his legs flexed and stretched behind him like a crane's in a Chinese painting. We watched, and then Terry paddled back to the dock. The canoe had three different loops of rope, and he fastened all of them.

"When he saw you before, he went *closer*," I said now. "I never saw a bird do that."

"I thought he was going to carry me away."

"You didn't really?"

He looked up. "In a way, for a second, I did."

The cabin's screen door banged and I turned around. Nina was coming down to the lake. She is not yet old but I saw that she descended the hill carefully, like an older woman, watching for rocks. A city dweller, she looked in both directions when she crossed the narrow dirt road, though there were never any cars. She is a thin, freckled woman with curly gray hair, and she was wearing a bathing suit and a red sweatshirt.

"It's gone," I called to her.

"What is?"

"The Great Blue Heron. Terry was almost carried off by a Great Blue Heron."

"He was? I couldn't hear what he said." She came down to the dock and took off her canvas shoes.

"Are you going swimming?" said Terry.

"I thought I might," Shoogie said, "but I've missed the sun. It's out there in the middle of the lake." The inlet where we were staying was so narrow that the evergreen trees alongside shaded it long before sunset.

"We could take the canoe out," I said. "We could chase the sun."

"That would be wonderful. I'd rather do that than swim." The canoe, wide and flat-bottomed, was easy to paddle, though I hadn't been in one since my childhood. It was big enough for three, but Terry was not interested, so Nina and I climbed in, she in front.

Nina lives in Boston and Terry and I in New York, but we talk on the phone every few weeks. "I've always liked you, Jo," she said when Mark and I separated. "I'm afraid this might be Mark's fault." I didn't think she meant that Mark had done something wrong. I thought she might mean he was boring.

"I'm hard to live with," I said. During the year of the divorce, I used to comfort myself with a list of my failings, which did seem to prove that the divorce was my fault— but somehow in a way that gave me satisfaction. I am hot-tempered, I'd point out to myself, and I'm overcautious and a bit driven. Mostly, I'm arrogant. Mark is one of those men women call teddy bears. At first, his sweet, loud slowness pleased me; then it didn't. I told myself that the marriage ended the first time I told a joke and he didn't get it. But though my own parents had agreed readily that I was hard to live with, Shoogie would never accept it. "You're not *cloying*, of course," she said.

We'd often discussed Mark—his jobs, his girlfriends. That spring she'd told me that she'd talked on the phone to a woman Mark was seeing, named Sarah. "Sensitive," she'd said in a prissy falsetto. Then, in her own voice, "I had to pick my words."

Mark recently moved to California, where Sarah lives. In the past, he'd often taken Terry to visit Nina, but now he's too far away, and Terry missed his grandmother. Then I thought of inviting her along on our vacation. She agreed and even found the place through an ad in the *Globe*. We shared the cost. I was pleased with myself—for having the idea, for not minding her.

Now I took my paddle and pushed away from the dock. When we turned the canoe, I could see a band of sunlight ahead of us, as if the lake were made of separately tinted strips of something.

"I haven't taken a vacation in years," Shoogie said, "except to go to New York. I spend my vacations in bed, noshing and reading. Of course, that's fun, too." Nina is a social worker at a hospital. Sometimes, on the phone, she begins wearily, "This is Saint Nina," and then tells me how she spent the day fighting some government office that had refused to help one of her clients. Her stories generally end, "So I just told off that supervisor, and lo and behold—success at last." Sometimes she adds, "You can't be meek and sweet in *this* job."

I steered the canoe toward the quietest part of the lake, the cove near ours where the heron had gone. When I'd canoed around the lake with Terry, I could see that there were many summer homes, but most of them seemed to be empty, though sometimes a motor boat would appear, making huge arcs from one dock or another, and a few times, from our porch, we'd seen a water skier, a small, brittle, upright shape with arms outstretched. It would circle again and again, and then fall—the figure would break in the middle and the boat would loop solicitously back toward it.

"So, listen, you know about Sarah?" said Nina, as we paddled toward the sunny water.

"What about her?"

"I think he's going to marry her." We reached the sunny part of the lake. It felt wonderful—as if something warm were suddenly poured over us—but the sun would be gone in a few minutes, and it was almost the end of August. For a moment I felt as if I were going to be cold for the rest of my life.

"You think so or he says so?" I asked. It annoyed me that Nina didn't speak precisely.

"Mark says he thinks so. I can't say I'm overjoyed."

"It's his business," I said, keeping my voice casual. "I hope they'll be happy."

"I'm sorry, Jo—I thought he told you. My big mouth, as usual."

"I don't care," I said. "You can tell me things. But no, I didn't know—Mark and I just talk about Terry."

"He should have told you," said Shoogie. Then, after a pause, she said, "He says you don't want Terry to visit him at Christmas."

Now I got angry. "I don't care about Terry visiting Mark," I said. "It's Terry alone in the airplane I object to."

"It's not unusual, at eleven," she said. "And by then he'll be almost twelve."

"Look, I'm afraid the plane will crash and my child will be killed," I said brutally. "Imagine Terry, sitting alone in a crashing plane, knowing he's going to die. Tell me it's impossible and I'll stop objecting."

I had pulled the paddle onto my knees and I saw that
Nina had done the same with hers. We were still, in the
middle of the lake, in the sun. Then I saw the heron again.
It was rising heavily above the trees, crossing the arm of
the lake.

"Look!" I said. "Did you see it?"

"Yes, yes, it's wonderful," said Nina.

I'd sounded excited when I saw the bird, and that made
me feel foolish for my outburst, as if I hadn't meant it.
When I stopped talking it was so quiet that it seemed as
if I'd screamed when I talked about planes, as if people
must have heard me—though I saw no signs of people. I
had meant it—yet I knew that in the end I would send
Terry on the plane.

"Would it help if I go with him?" Nina said.

"No." It wouldn't help. But by the logic I'd just used,
she was offering to risk her life.

She didn't speak for a long time, and I thought she was
angry with me. Then she said, "Jo, of course I can't say
it's *impossible*."

"I know."

We both picked up our paddles again and I tried to turn
the canoe. We'd drifted almost to the opposite shore, and
now we had to go all the way back against the wind—it
had gotten windier. It was chilly, and soon it would
be time for supper. I couldn't see our own deep cove,
but I knew that as soon as I passed a rock that jutted
out into the lake not very far away, it would open out on
our left. I dipped the paddle over and over into water that
had been broken by the wind into tiny facets, like a
transparent, shiny piece of paper that has been creased

into many even squares, but that constantly heaves and shifts.

It took a long time. We were silent, then talked again. Without knowing why, I asked, "How come you don't like Sarah?"

"Oh, she's—" Nina shrugged one shoulder irritably. "She doesn't have your sense of humor, for one thing."

"I don't either," I said. "It dried up."

Nina snorted. "She's too nice."

At last we reached the point where the rock was, and then I could see our dock—a tiny, crooked line—and a mustard-colored spot that was a tarp covering a motor boat belonging to the owners of the cabin. Our cove was so narrow that it looked like evening there; the pine trees made great black shadows on the water.

"I guess Terry went up to the cabin," Nina said. I couldn't see him either. Then a black pickup truck appeared on the dirt road below our cabin and stopped. I watched the truck, surprised—I hadn't seen more than a car or two all day—and then I saw a small figure in white, who had to be Terry, now in his T-shirt, come out of our cabin and move down the hill toward the truck.

"Where did that truck come from?" Nina said.

"I don't know." There were trees and bushes between the cabin and the truck, and after Terry passed the open part of the hill, where there was a flight of wooden steps, I could no longer see him.

"Can you see Terry now?" I asked.

"No." We were both paddling faster. Nina's short arms thrust the paddle at the water again and again. I aimed at the truck, stretching my paddle toward it. Drops swung out in an arc as the paddle came toward the water.

"He wouldn't do anything foolish, would he?" said Nina.

"You mean get into the truck? Of course not." But I wasn't certain, and now the truck moved slowly again into the woods on the other side of the cabin. I couldn't see Terry, but I didn't have a complete view because of the trees. I knew how unlikely it was that any harm could come to him, far in the country in Maine, but it was not my home, it was not what I am used to.

"I'm sure he's in the trees," said Nina.

"You see him?"

"No."

Neither of us spoke for a long time—we were paddling hard—and then Nina said, "Mark actually did that once," and glanced over her shoulder at me. "See, I can talk about it to you," she said. "You're not some unrealistic ninny."

"What happened?"

"He was ten," said Nina. "I sent him to the store, and I didn't give him enough money. When he went to the counter to pay, he was twenty cents short. There was a man waiting behind him, and as soon as he saw what had happened, he put two dimes down on the counter and pushed them next to Mark's money. So Mark got confused, and when the man insisted on giving him a ride home, he went. And the man parked on a quiet street and stuck his hand down Mark's pants." She stopped. Her voice had the false, bitter lightness she sometimes used when she talked about her clients' troubles.

"What happened then?" I said. Mark had never told me this story.

"We were lucky, I guess," said Nina. "He was able to open the door and run home. He left the groceries on the front seat. If it wasn't for that, he might never have told me."

I didn't know what to say. I didn't say anything, I just kept moving the canoe along as fast as I could, and after a while Terry, in his white shirt, emerged from the trees and crossed the beach. He was coming out onto the dock. We'd made progress—I could see him clearly now.

"Look," I said.

"Of course," said Nina. "We were silly to worry, but I guess it was the wrong time to tell you that story!"

"Your stories don't bother me," I said. I didn't want to remind her of Sarah. "You're like grapefruit juice," I added, "but I *like* grapefruit juice."

"I'm like what?" She turned her head.

"Grapefruit juice."

She turned back with a short laugh and waved at Terry, and he waved back. He put something up to his face. It was the binoculars.

After a while she said, "Mark was different from Terry, but still, he was only ten." I knew what she meant when she said Mark was different. Terry was small for his age, and somewhat shy, while I was sure Mark had always been big and confident. He is a little overweight now, but that isn't the reason he seems to take up most of the space in a room. He stands with his legs spread farther apart than other people's, and when he arrives someplace he positions himself just beyond the edge of what's happening—in a doorway, maybe—but then talks to people all over the room. That was how we met—he started talking to me at an office party, with a dozen people between us. "Have you tried these big shrimps?" he called, pointing to the table of food, and I knew he was aiming the remark at me. Still, there had always been something else about Mark—a way of paying attention as if he always expected to hear something that might be hard for him to understand—and when I thought of him at ten, it was that listening look I pictured.

Terry got tired of following our slow progress and went back up to the cabin. By then, though, we were almost there. I was concentrating on guiding the canoe in—a dead tree stuck out into the water and we had to go between it and the dock—but I was also imagining a city street, and Mark, a boy, running home from the man. He would always have run the way he does now. He seems to run in all directions, the way a baby does, with a great churning of the air. And now he was running away from me and toward Sarah, who would be his new wife.

My arms stiff with effort, I brought the boat in. It was important to stop Mark. I'd wanted him all along, I thought—it had been a misunderstanding. I told myself the old reasons why he and I were better off apart, but I wasn't convinced this time. Finally the canoe bumped against the dock. It was damp and cold in the cove, and the water was black. I leaned over to throw the loops of rope around the upright two-by-fours nailed to the dock to receive them, and something broke in me. I changed position, put down the paddle, climbed onto the dock on my knees, chilled and tired, and stayed that way, on my hands and knees. I didn't stand up, didn't turn around and help Nina out—she had to do a sort of belly flop to scramble out of the canoe. I remembered the first time Mark and I had slept together. We'd known each other a few weeks.

It was an awkward, quiet occasion that turned out full of laughter. With a golden, fierce intensity that I hugged close, because I might never feel it again, I *objected* to the marriage of Mark and Sarah. He was my husband. I had his mother and his child. I could stretch my arms wide and put a finger on each end of Mark's life.

C H U N K Y

B R A C E L E T S

Katya was hot from walking. She unlocked the balky door of her shop and took off her two sweat-shirts—a thin blue one and a new, thick, pink one, silkscreened with luscious purple flowers, which Richard had bought her—flung them both off in one economical gesture that made her feel free, cool, and even young and slim (unencumbered, bare-armed in a T-shirt), though she wasn't any of those things. It was Sunday. Her store would be closed until noon, and she had come to straighten up, count shirts and socks, and look over a new shipment of cotton jackets. And to be alone. And to talk to Jonas if he came along.

The phone rang. It would be Richard. "Alive," said Katya, picking up the receiver, "despite half-mile walk to State Street. Blood pressure normal, pulse normal . . ." What if it were somebody else?

"That's not why I called," said Richard, though he did laugh. "It's over a mile, though. You forgot your lunch. Shall I bring it over?"

"Oh—all right." It was his idea that she take along a nourishing, nonfattening lunch instead of sending out for coffee and a sub from the deli, which she liked better. He'd even offered to get it ready, and then she'd walked out without giving it a thought.

Her store sold women's clothing, much of it in red, yellow, purple. She had been a nursery school teacher until her mother died, leaving her enough money to start this business, and apparently the colors of the preschool classroom had lodged in Katya's soul. Her mother, who wore gray, would have been startled—and there was her name over the door, too: Hannah's, the store was called. People asked if Katya was Hannah. "Her daughter," she said. And her mother, soon—at thirty-nine, Katya was pregnant for the first time. The doctor had called on Friday with the results of the amniocentesis. "No problems," she'd said, "and it's a girl."

"Hannah," Katya had replied, welcoming this surprise daughter who'd come after she'd tried to get pregnant for years. At low, crazy times she'd imagined that she'd given her mother-love away to other people's Daniels and Hannahs and didn't have enough left to make her own baby. Maybe it was true—maybe this year of happy mourning had helped the new Hannah come into being while Katya filled her racks with color and encouraged her customers to wear it. There was even an older woman with blue eyes and clear skin who looked something like Katya's mother, and she'd begun to wear the blues and greens in which she was beautiful. But the store wasn't making a profit.

Katya began to look over the new jackets. Some were a clear orange, almost coral. The seams were carefully finished. Now she heard a patter of fingernails on the glass door. It was not Jonas but his girlfriend, Roz, carrying a brown paper bag with her latest bracelets. She'd been after Katya to take some on consignment.

Roz was younger than Katya and a lot younger than Jonas, who had been selling secondhand furniture and antiques down the street for years, since he'd fried his brains, he said, on LSD in the sixties and dropped out of college. He'd gone to work for an old man whose sons weren't interested in the business; eventually, Jonas took it over. Roz had been his girlfriend for just a few months. She had frizzy hair that hung over her eyes; it—or something—gave her a disdainful look, and yet she always seemed ready to cry.

"I took your advice," she said in her quavery voice when Katya opened the door.

"Hi," said Katya. Roz's bracelets were made of shells, large irregular beads, and rough stones. Katya thought they would cut into the wrist. These new ones, she saw, had even bigger stones.

"I added feathers," Roz said, "and these little silky braided things."

She fastened a bracelet on Katya's arm, and Katya tensed. "Wear it to something important," Roz said. "Then when it goes badly, like, you'll have something to grab onto." Katya imagined herself in labor, running her fingers on Roz's grotesque blocks and beads.

"It's cool if you don't want to take them."

Katya wanted to get the bracelets out of her shop, but she said yes. She couldn't think of how not to with Roz facing her, her child's face held still as if with the effort not to let it crumple, her eyes cynical. Katya scooped bracelets out of the bag and arranged them under her glass-topped counter. Roz left, looking negative anyway, folding her empty grocery bag. Under the glass countertop, the stones and shells seemed to spell out a message: Stay away from Jonas.

Not that Katya wanted Jonas. It had been a topic of conversation between her and Richard for months—how hard Jonas would be to live with. He'd shown up right after they'd taken the lease on the store and helped Katya paint and set up. He was full of advice. "Advice! He's a bully," Katya had said, but she could hear the affection in her voice. She looked for excuses to talk about Jonas. "The big bad antiques man came by again today," she'd say. "He says I have no business instincts."

"He certainly speaks his mind," Richard would reply.

Jonas had told her to hang some dresses and shirts flat against the wall, instead of keeping them all on racks. "This is your best fall item," he'd said about a plaid dress in gold and black that Katya had had her doubts about. "It's the only thing in the store that's the least bit inter-esting. Put it where people can see it." She'd hung five identical gold-and-black dresses in a row on the wall, and he was right: the item had done well. "It's the length," Jonas said. "Women like you to see the backs of their knees. Women think the backs of their knees are their sexiest spot. Such vulnerable little indentations."

For a while during the winter, Jonas was distant and quiet. He hardly ever came over. But he'd been his old self from the day Roz first turned up—a customer who'd come into his store to buy a lamp for her bedroom. "The pussy shortage is over," he'd announced, coming into Katya's shop one morning. Katya had been embarrassed.

Roz's bracelet got in Katya's way when she was straightening up, and she took it off. She was waiting for Jonas, she realized (while also waiting for Richard, and wondering why he hadn't shown up with her lunch, and hoping they wouldn't come at the same time), just so she could have a fight with him about Roz, and sure enough, when Jonas came she quarreled with him, though she was in the wrong, and he pointed that out.

"You could have said no. Who are you doing a favor? What do you think, she's never heard the word no before?"

"I couldn't."

"So what's wrong with the bracelets?"

"I don't know. I don't like them."

"You don't have such an infallible eye, you know," said Jonas. "They might take off."

"They seem dated," she said, pretending to be more rational than she felt.

"Bullshit," he said. "This is the latest thing. What do *you* know?" He was leaning on the counter, pressing his hands into the glass above the display of bracelets. When he moved his hands, she watched his fingerprints, as detailed as for a detective's files, to see if they'd disappear.

"Admit it—you don't like them either," she said, feeling reckless. "You don't like *any* of Roz's work." Then she touched his bare arm, because he looked at her without speaking and she wondered if she'd gone too far.

"I don't know what you're talking about," he said. He was short but barrel-chested, and his arms were big.

"Yes, you do."

"No," he said, and this time he sounded angry and tired.

"I don't know what you've got against Roz. We're having enough problems—" He paused, then continued. "And I don't know why nothing is simple for you, Katya. You're spoiled. You got the money for this business handed to you on a silver platter, and you think it's a game—one thing is dated, another one gives you a bad feeling. I'm tired of it. I'm going."

"Wait," said Katya as he opened the door.

"Other people don't have husbands with fancy jobs," he said. "Other people have to earn their living." The door closed behind him.

It was almost time to open the store. Katya was hungry. She was annoyed with Richard, who hadn't brought her lunch but had made it impossible for her to buy a different lunch. She tried to tell herself it was hunger and Richard that made her feel uneasy and upset. Fights with Jonas were ordinary.

She didn't think she was spoiled. She'd worked hard this year, and hard at the nursery school all the years before that. Richard, a city planner, worked hard too. There was nothing glamorous about his job. She wanted to say all this to Jonas. She found herself moving her lips, defending herself and Richard in an imaginary conversation.

She felt the baby move inside her. She was just beginning to be certain it was the baby she felt, not just a gas bubble. This was a real kick. She put her hand on her stomach and waited. She was beginning to show. Under her shirt her belly was tight and round. For some weeks now, she'd had to wear pants with elastic waists. Not many of the clothes in the store would fit her.

When the store opened, two customers came in right

away, women Katya didn't know. She could tell they were good friends. They began examining the merchandise and talking about it. "This would be good on you," one said, holding up a sundress. "I don't have the bosom for it." The other came over to look.

Then Richard arrived, carrying her little canvas tote bag with its thermos bottle, container of yogurt, and banana. "I parked in a driveway down the street," he said, opening the door. "Nobody's going to care, will they, as long as I'm quick?"

"I don't know," said Katya. Richard, six three, always ducked his head slightly coming through a doorway, like a vassal giving a nervous bow to an exacting lord. He didn't quite fill up his height. She sometimes wished she could press down on the top of his head to shorten and thicken him.

It was not like him to park in a driveway. "I was afraid if I didn't get here, you'd eat junk." He studied nutrition charts these days. He was running with the tote bag, holding it out toward Katya.

"What took you so long?"

"I had to go to the hardware store before it closed, and it took a full hour," he said. "I was certain your yogurt would spoil out in the car."

"I'm sure it's fine." This lunch would not fill her. She was always hungry now. She'd probably get a cinnamon bun from the bakery later in the afternoon if it was quiet in the store. Or she'd send Jonas for one if they were still speaking.

"I had a fight with Jonas," she said.

"That's nothing new."

"Well, it was different," she said.

"What happened?"

"Oh, I don't know," she said. "It's hard to explain." The two women came forward to pay for some socks and left the store.

"There was a pregnant woman in the hardware store," said Richard. "She was gigantic. You won't be like that. She obviously hadn't taken care of herself."

"That has nothing to do with it," said Katya sharply.

"Of course it does."

"Richard, that's not true."

She stepped out from behind the counter and walked over to a shelf of T-shirts. The pile was disheveled, and she refolded several shirts. One of Roz's bracelets was lying on the shelf next to the shirts, the one she had put on Katya's arm. Katya had left it there when she took it off. Now she fastened it on her wrist again. It had several ridged amber beads, and a block of what looked like driftwood.

The door opened—it was Jonas. "Richard," he called, "they're towing your car."

Richard turned on him. "But I've been here less than five minutes!"

"What can I tell you? *I'm* not towing it," said Jonas. Now Katya could hear the toot of a tow truck backing up. Richard hurried out of the store, and Katya followed him. Standing next to their car was a policeman writing a ticket. The men with the tow truck were fastening the cables to their car.

Katya stayed in the doorway while Richard had an argument with the policeman, who was calm at first, then got angry. He sent away the tow truck but gave Richard a ticket. Richard couldn't handle it; he couldn't stop arguing.

Katya was afraid he'd cry. Finally Jonas appeared, said something to the cop, and escorted Richard around his car to the driver's side. Richard drove away and Jonas spoke with the cop for another moment and then went back into his store.

The policeman got into his car and drove away, too. Suddenly, after the commotion, Katya was alone on the street. She stood there in the silence, trying to calm herself. The sun was shining and the day was just a bit cool. She leaned on a parked car in front of her store. She could look down the street and see Jonas's store, and after a while he came out. He was coming over to her.

"Your husband was lucky," he said. "That cop was thinking about arresting him."

"What did you say to him?" She sounded strange to herself. She wanted to tell him she wasn't spoiled.

"I told the cop Richard was a foreign prince. That he wasn't used to our ways."

She laughed, and for a while they were silent. She saw him notice the bracelet, but he didn't say anything, and neither did she. He leaned on the car next to her in the sun, and then after a while she went back into the store and he followed her. Opening the door, she brushed against his bare arm. He was sweaty. She remembered how in the nursery school there were always some children who felt warmer to the touch than others, who were like little furnaces when she held them on her lap in warm weather.

"I think Miss Roz is getting tired of me," Jonas said. He sat down on Katya's chair behind the counter. He looked older than usual. His sandy hair had more gray in it than she'd realized.

"Oh, no," she said quickly, then, "Why do you say that?"

"At first, her favorite thing was spending Sunday afternoon at the store with me," he said. "With one hand down my pants, behind a bookcase. Today, she stayed for a few minutes—looking bored—and then announced she was going to the beach with her girlfriend. Picked up her little ass and took off."

"She'll come back," said Katya. She wondered whether he *loved* Roz—in just what way he minded this. If Roz were her lover, she would want her to stop looking as if she were about to cry and to stop looking critical, or at least to explain how she could look both those things at once. Jonas didn't seem to think about this question.

"That was quite a scene—your man trying to scare away the cop," he was saying.

"I don't know why that happened," said Katya. It had given her great pain to see Richard that way, but maybe she asked too much of him. Maybe she ought to think of him the way Jonas thought of Roz. She liked going to bed with Richard. He was a conscientious lay, she thought, and wished she could say that to Jonas. Richard would work to get her to come. He was already reading up on sex in late pregnancy.

"I bet it's his first parking ticket," said Jonas. "I bet he never even got a parking ticket before."

"That's possible," said Katya. "I can't remember. I've certainly had plenty."

"He's *got* to protest his first ticket. And whatever it costs," he said, "it's that much less for his kid. He's got to have money for the kid, you know. Can't depend on this store bringing it in."

He looked around at Katya's summery display of T-shirts and shorts and sundresses, and she followed his gaze. Any moment now, the store might be jammed with customers. There were days when it happened. But the whole street was in trouble; she knew that Jonas's business wasn't having a good year. When the baby came, she'd have to close for a while, or hire an assistant, whom she couldn't afford. She had imagined working in the store after Hannah was born, bringing the baby in a wicker basket with a brightly checked hood, but now she wasn't sure that would be possible. Jonas was straightening some of the hanging clothes. He had to stretch to reach the ones on the wall. He wasn't much taller than Katya.

She would be huge in this pregnancy. Her mother, the family story had gone, was so big when she was pregnant with Katya that everyone assumed she was carrying twins. Walking down the street in her eighth month, Hannah had been hailed by a bus driver who stopped his bus in mid-block, opened the doors, and jumped out to offer her a ride. And Katya was just her mother's height, with her mother's squarish build.

"It's a tough world, lady," said Jonas, and Katya thought that although he'd said what everyone said, *she'd* never believed it. She'd always expected things to improve presently. The people who didn't understand would catch on— amazed that it had taken them so long—and repairs would be undertaken, and sooner or later joy would come unalloyed by pain. She saw Jonas looking at her hands. She was running her fingers over the ridges in one of Roz's beads. She laughed and dropped her arms to her sides.

"Sweet lady," said Jonas. He came over to her and put his hands on her shoulders. Then they each leaned forward, and they pressed their foreheads together. His was moist. Katya and Jonas were almost the same height, both a little bulky. He let his arms fall and they stood that way, eyes closed, at rest, letting their thoughts even out. Some of hers needed to make their way into his mind, while some of his came to her.

THE

FLIGHT

OF

ANDY BURNS

At the last minute there isn't enough spaghetti
and Jack runs out to the corner store. He's a hero,
everyone says, because it's raining and there's a
big wind, but when he steps out into the rain it
excites him—wild, energetic weather, not too
cold. Rain sometimes induces a kind of euphoria
in Jack, whose life has gone well lately, but he
thinks that when people are sad rain probably
makes it worse.

When he steps into the store his glasses fog
up immediately, and he has to stop and rub them
on the hem of his coat. The store is bright and
warm; it's a tiny neighborhood grocery that was
recently taken over by new people, who have
added a deli in the back and a display of herbal
teas. Jack would like to buy something festive for
the company at his house tonight, and after a
search he settles on homemade noodles, which

the store has also started carrying lately. He buys two large packages of them. They do not lie flat, like the noodles in boxes; they take up a lot of room. On the way home he must hold his brown paper bag carefully, not to crush them. His raincoat billows out behind him because of the wind.

The visitors at his house are his cousin Susan and her husband, Ray. They are stopping here in New Haven tonight just to have dinner with Jack and his family, and then they'll drive on to Boston to visit their son, who is a graduate student at Tufts. They live in New Jersey, and they've been on the road for most of the afternoon. Later, there will be another guest—Ray's brother Mickey, whom Jack has never met. Mickey has recently moved to New Haven, and he will be coming over for dessert.

Walking home, with the rain blowing in his face, Jack laughs at himself a little, because he sees that he'd like to do something big for his cousin and her husband, and noodles are all he's come up with. Susan and Ray have had trouble. A year ago, their daughter died of cancer—their older child, who was twenty-four. Jack tries to imagine how such a loss would feel after a year. Maybe at times one would even forget it altogether, forget that it happened, and then suddenly be reminded—or maybe not. It might be an awareness behind everything else, like a constant flickering light that turns the people and furniture in a room into incomplete, interrupted shapes.

When Jack opens the door of his house he hears his older son (and middle child), Philip, playing his guitar and singing "Union Maid." Everyone is in the kitchen.

Ray is standing in the kitchen doorway with his back to Jack, and Jack hears him join lustily in the chorus—"Oh, you can't scare me, I'm sticking to the union. . . ." Ray is scooping his arms up and forward enthusiastically, as if a large crowd of shy people behind him must be encouraged to join in the singing. Jack, who is actually behind him, does join in softly—he's shy about singing—while setting his parcel on a small table in the hall and taking off his wet raincoat. At the end of the song he carries the big bag of noodles into the kitchen. "We usually have to wait for dessert to hear Philip," he says.

"Tonight I'm the appetizer," says Philip.

"He's helping me distract the guests from the fact that they haven't been fed yet," says Franny, Jack's wife. There are crackers and cheese on the table, and all the adults except Ray are drinking wine. Ray is a beer drinker. Franny looks into the spaghetti pot on the stove and turns up the flame under it. She opens one of the packages of noodles.

"Make enough, Mom," says Martin. He is thirteen, their youngest child. Stephanie, the oldest, a high-school junior, is sitting next to Susan, talking earnestly to her in a low voice. Her head is bent and the reflection of the overhead light makes an oval on her smooth, short brown hair. Jack is glad she's there. He can't help wanting Susan and Ray to see what she's like, even while fearing that she may remind them of Becky, their daughter. But Stephanie isn't staying, it seems; she brushes past him and goes into the other room, then returns in her coat. She's going to a meeting, he remembers now. She's in a group that is helping to organize a rally on the New Haven Green for the homeless. That must be what she was talking about to Susan.

"Where's the meeting?" Jack asks her.

"Maple Street," says Stephanie. He still isn't used to her being old enough to drive. "I'll stop for all the red lights," she says. "*And* the stop signs. 'Bye, everyone."

Susan blows her a kiss. "She's so grown up," she says. She turns toward Philip. "You, too. How do you like high school? Isn't this your first year?"

"It's OK," says Philip. "I don't like gym, though."

He glances at Franny, who says to him, "Believe it or not, I made some progress today, but is it OK to talk about it?"

"Sure," says Philip calmly, to Jack's surprise. Philip explains that he is the shortest boy in gym class, and the others make fun of him. Once someone punched him. He'd like to get permission to drop gym and take it next year, when he'll surely be bigger, but apparently only parents can make that sort of thing happen.

"I've been leaving messages for that guidance counselor, but we keep missing each other," says Franny. She is draining the noodles now. "Finally she had someone give me her home phone number. I'm going to call her after supper." She ladles chicken, broccoli, and mushrooms into the bowl.

Philip doesn't seem short to Jack. In the last couple of years, all his children have been transformed as if by magic from creatures he could pick up easily to people whose jackets he can borrow, at least for a one-minute dash out-side—as mighty a change, it seems, as could possibly occur. Strangely, it has also made the children seem even more fragile than they used to be; when they were small, he remembers now, he would sometimes picture himself slipping them into his pocket.

He stands up to help Franny carry the food to the table, and Philip puts his guitar back into its case. When Jack sits down again, there is a brief silence. "So how are you doing?" he says, as they all pull their chairs closer.

"Well, it hasn't been my favorite year," says Susan.

Jack nods, and then nods again, a little differently, to encourage her to help herself from the bowl of noodles and chicken and vegetables.

"But it wasn't as bad as the year before that," she goes on. "That was the worst time, when the news was always bad."

Susan passes the bowl on to Ray. "This looks great," he says. "Becky used to play the guitar," he says to Philip. "I remember her playing Joan Baez songs. Do you know those?"

"Some," says Philip. Now he is shyer.

"When I was your age I was shorter than you," Ray says.

Philip smiles. Ray, who is the head of a real-estate firm in New Brunswick, is a middle-sized man now, but he seems larger. He has broad shoulders and powerful arms and a loud, cheerful voice. Now he gestures with his napkin as he raises it to his lips. "They punched you?"

"Sort of," says Philip.

"Big guys?"

"Pretty big."

"And they pass remarks?"

"Sometimes."

Ray turns to Franny. "You're doing the right thing not to leave it alone," he says.

.

"My brother needs a ride," says Ray. They have finished eating, and the children have gone upstairs. Ray has been leaning back in his chair listening while Franny and Susan talk. Susan hasn't said much except to ask Franny questions about the children. "I'll go get Mickey," Ray says, getting up. He goes out to the hall to find his raincoat, and when he comes back he's holding an umbrella. "Can I borrow this?" he says. "But I don't know what good it'll do. The wind will just turn it inside out."

There's a sudden push of wind as he goes out and then slams the door behind him. Franny excuses herself to go and call the guidance counselor. Jack finds himself alone in the kitchen with Susan. He sets about clearing the table, not very fast. He shouldn't rush around noisily, he feels, but if he sat and looked at Susan that wouldn't be good, either. He would like to be useful to her.

"Are you teaching this year?" he says as he begins to gather up the silverware.

Susan had been a dancer when she was younger; more recently she has taught in a ballet school. She's gained weight, but she's still shapely and graceful. She's a little taller than her husband. Her clothes look soft to him to-night—gray slacks, a loose pink sweater with a gray scarf that's arranged near her face.

Susan tells him that lately she has been selling real estate in Ray's firm. Before that, she had been home too much. "Thinking," she says. "The school I taught in just wasn't open for many hours altogether. Now I can sit in the office, if I need to, and see people."

"Are you selling houses or business properties?" Jack

looks over his shoulder at her. She looks dignified—credible. Customers would trust her, he decides.

"Some of each," she says. "And I've been renovating an old house with another woman—that's the best part."

"That's wonderful."

"Yes. We've tiled a bathroom and hung wallpaper and painted. I never did those things before."

"I think that's great," he says.

"When we began, I kept *assuming* things would go wrong," Susan goes on. "When I painted, I expected the paint to just peel away from the wall in little strips." She pauses. Jack has found a refrigerator dish and is spooning the leftover noodles into it. "I used to be an optimist," Susan says.

"I guess you'd have to be, to dance." He is thinking of turns and leaps, of hurling oneself into the air.

But before Susan can answer, Franny comes into the room, looking pleased. "Wait till you hear about this guidance counselor!" she says. "I explained about the gym class. I said maybe we were making too much of it, but she just said, 'Well, I'll yank him out!' Just like that— 'I'll *yank* him out!' " She smiles at them both. "She sounded like Ethel Merman."

Philip is behind her. "Rescued!" he says, smiling at Susan.

When Ray and Mickey arrive a few minutes later—they come in laughing, pummeled by the wind and rain—they, too, must hear about the guidance counselor. Mickey turns out to be younger than Ray: slighter, with an elfin look. He doesn't seem to mind hearing about Philip and the gym class, even though he's just barely come through the door. " 'I'll yank him out!' " Philip repeats with satisfaction.

"I need someone like that in *my* life," Mickey says. He gives Jack his damp raincoat, and they all sit down at the table. There are cookies and ice cream for dessert, and when everyone has been served Franny sets about making coffee. "I have decaffeinated, too," she says, taking the mugs out of the cupboard.

"I'd better have the real stuff," Ray says. "We still have a long drive."

"All right if I fall asleep in the car?" Susan says to him.

"Sure," he says. "You sleep, I'll drive."

When the coffee is ready, Jack jumps up to carry the full mugs to the table. They are dark-blue mugs, almost black, made by a potter they once knew. "With caffeine," he says to Ray—he is being careful to keep track. Then he gives Mickey his. But when he is setting Susan's mug down on the table next to her, either his hand shakes or she moves for some reason and jerks her arm against the mug—Jack thinks later that he might have seen her arm move—and the mug tips over, splashing hot coffee on Susan's thighs, and then rolls to the edge of the table and falls to the floor. Susan jumps up and cries out, and then she is sobbing—a startling, terrible sound—while Jack grabs a dish towel and swipes at her legs, but Franny calls sharply, "Take off your pants!" She pushes Susan toward the hall and into the bathroom, while Susan, still crying, starts to fumble with her belt buckle. By the time Franny gets her into the bathroom Susan has pulled her pants down. Franny splashes cold water on Susan's thighs, Jack sees from the hall—he is following them—and then he thinks to back away. "Are you all right?" he keeps calling. "Are you all right?"

"She'll be all right," says Ray. He has picked up the mug—the handle has broken off—and he and Philip are sopping up coffee with paper towels.

"Put wet towels on her legs," Mickey calls.

"I am," Franny says. She keeps the water running in the basin, keeping the towels cold, and after a while Susan calls out, "I'm OK. It's all right. But my pants are soaked."

Ray goes out to the car and brings in their suitcase. "It's still raining," he says. "Still so windy, too."

When Susan comes out of the bathroom wearing a different pair of pants—blue, this time—Jack puts his arms around her. "I am *so* sorry," he says. She hugs him back, hard. He has always liked Susan, but he cannot remember hugging her before, even when they visited her and Ray last year just after Becky died. They kissed then, he seems to recollect, but they didn't hug.

"It's all right," says Susan. "It only hurts a little. And I liked being looked after." Then she turns to Ray. "I really am fine—but it's late. We have to go."

It *is* late, everyone suddenly notices. Ray takes a last mouthful of coffee—Susan never did get her decaffeinated, Franny points out—and he and Mickey stand up together and each smiles at the other. Franny has been sponging the gray slacks; now she puts them into a plastic bag for Susan while Jack goes for the visitors' coats.

"We'll drop you off," Ray says to Mickey. "It's right on the way, practically." They all move into the front hall, talking, and when Ray opens the door they can still hear the wind.

Jack is holding Susan's coat for her. "Now, don't blow away!" he says.

"Good point," says Mickey, and he suddenly beams at Jack as if he'd said something particularly sharp. "When I was in fifth grade—in Mrs. Corelli's room— Remember her, Ray?"

"Sure," says Ray.

"You wouldn't fool around with Mrs. Corelli," says Mickey. "Anyway, one day it was windy and rainy, just like this, and a boy named Andy Burns came to school and announced to the whole class that on his way the wind picked him up and blew him kitty-corner across the street and then set him down again, right on his route."

"Did that really *happen*?" says Martin.

Jack pictures a ten-year-old floating across a busy intersection—he pictures a crossing near his house, where the store is, actually.

"The thing is, he just wasn't the sort of boy who'd make it up," says Mickey. "He was shy and very serious. He didn't usually talk that way at *all*—you know, stand up and say something to the whole class."

"Unlike you, I'm sure," says Susan, smiling, though her eyes are still red from crying. "I'm sure you talked all the time, and made things up, too."

"Oh, I was awful," says Mickey.

"Did he use the word *kitty-corner*?" Franny asks.

"Yes," says Mickey. "Somehow I've always thought he wouldn't make that part up."

He turns back as they head for the door. "But don't worry—I'll hold on to Susan and Ray." He puts one hand lightly on each of them, on their shoulders, while everyone says good-bye, and as they all three start down the porch steps, still with Mickey's hands on the others' shoulders,

The Flight of Andy Burns

Jack lets himself imagine that his cousin and her husband will indeed be lifted off their feet by the wind. Held fast by Mickey, they will stream out behind him in the air like beginning swimmers learning the flutter kick. The wind won't hurt them or carry them away—it will just give them a ride.

THE

HAWK

ON THE

FENCE

I'm worried because I've heard that I won't be allowed to take my bag inside, that I'll have to leave it at the desk and carry in only the books of poems from which I'm going to read aloud. But sometimes I need to put on my sunglasses, even indoors, if there are bright lights. What if I need to blow my nose or suck on a throat lozenge?

The bag is large, made of blue canvas. But no one mentions it. The librarian, a man with curly hair and a slightly upturned face, comes promptly to meet me. We walk through a corridor, then an empty auditorium, then out again into the sun and along a concrete walk. It's still hot, though it's six in the evening. "The buildings are air-conditioned," the librarian says. I hadn't expected that.

We cross a yard where men sit at picnic tables, or stand, talking. Brown buildings behind them have peaked roofs like houses, but too few features, like houses in Monopoly. The men are all in white T-shirts and dark pants: a picnic, but stylized, as if painted by an artist of a certain school whose name I can't remember—a school that omits detail. Two tight round beds of flowers are near the path—reds, yellows—but I find myself looking away, as if I'm not supposed to notice them.

The librarian and I go into the library, and then he leads me to a small room off the main one. It's about twelve feet long, and at one end is a freestanding blackboard on which my name is written in large letters. Nobody's there. In front of the blackboard is a padded metal desk chair with casters. The librarian motions me to that chair, but I sit down on one of the others—steel office chairs with red seats—in the middle of a row along one wall. On a small table in a corner are Styrofoam cups, a jar of instant coffee, and a white enamel kettle.

A man comes in and sits down. He looks like someone who might come from the gas company to install a new meter in the basement; he's about sixty. He says his name is Walter. "And what do *you* do for excitement?" he asks me.

"Oh, I don't know," I say, too brightly.

The second man has a broad, amused, battered face and carries books. He tells me that the books are about the war in Vietnam. "We have to learn about Vietnam," he says. "So many people died there."

I nod. "Sometimes they had to eat the bark off trees," says the man. "Before this, I read about World War Two."

Some of the men fix themselves instant coffee. The librarian has gone out but comes back with more water. He offers me coffee. "Sure," I say.

"Cream? Sugar?" The librarian says he isn't good at making coffee and I wonder whether I should have made it for myself.

"Where are the Fig Newtons?" says a man. "Did you run out?"

The librarian laughs. "You guys won't believe this," he says, turning around and spreading his open hands. "I went to the store, and when I got there, I had no money!" His face changes when he laughs; there is a hint of joy, actually, at finding, inside him (yet *again*)—himself!

He stirs nondairy creamer into my cup. "This is Michael," he tells me. "Herb. Stanfield. Billy." The men have all sat down. The librarian goes out again and closes the door. I wait while two more men come in and sit down. I don't want to stare at the men, so I look at one man's sneakers—high-top white sneakers with red stars on their sides and the words *All Star*. I see that all the other men have plain black leather shoes, a few pairs scuffed, most new and shined. The shoes, combined with the T-shirts, make the men look like lawyers on their day off, or maybe uncles . . . my idea of uncles.

"Aren't you going to sit in the comfortable chair?" asks Billy, a black man, maybe thirty.

"I'm fine here," I say. "If I sat in the chair with wheels, I'd scoot around."

"Then I'll sit in it," says Billy.

·

"I honestly don't know where poems *come* from," I say.

"From feelings you remember," says someone.

"I know," I say. "But some things just lie there in your

mind. In the dark." I look to see whether they know what I'm talking about. "And others are—well, lit up—"

"Sometimes you write to hide a feeling," Billy says from the wheeled chair. I begin to read poems aloud—one about someone walking home from a hospital after visiting a friend with cancer, and watching crazy teenagers hanging out in the cold; another about a couple in bed, waked at three in the morning when the alarm goes off by mistake. When the people in the poem speak, I let loose, and after I have read a few, a man hands me a piece of paper. "Read *my* poem," he says. "I want to hear how you'd read it." I'm wary, but I read it aloud anyway. It's a love poem, much rhymed, hinting at hardship. Then I return to the poems I've brought. One, as I read it, seems wrong. I sense bafflement around me. "Weird poem," I say, and the audience laughs. One is about a woman threatened with prison, and the men want to know if she had to go.

.

When the men write, I think I ought to write too. I take a notebook and pencil from my bag—this is what I needed from it—and write, "Brown buildings with fields between them. Small buildings that look something like barns or houses, something like barracks." But I'm self-conscious, and I put away the notebook. The men write for a long time and then stop, one by one. Finally no one is writing but the man next to me, and then he stops too. I tell them that reading aloud something so new would be hard for me. But the man with the books volunteers. Before reading, he says he was supposed to be given a furlough to visit his girlfriend. "I'm forty-four and this is my first time," he says. "They say if you can't do the time, you shouldn't do the crime. . . ." He shakes his head. "I got a traffic ticket, and now I can't go."

"A traffic ticket?" I say.

"A bad mark. I was wearing used shoes."

"What?"

"Someone else's shoes."

"You can't go because of your *shoes*?" The men all nod patiently, smiling at me. Now the man reads his piece aloud. It's a rhymed poem. It's funny—he rhymes *wise-crack* and *sacroiliac*. I can't get over it. He writes about shoes and a traffic ticket, but obscurely, so I wouldn't know what had happened if he hadn't begun by telling the story. When he finishes, he says he has written something serious that day for the first time. It's a message to his girlfriend. It's on a greeting card, which he takes carefully out of its envelope. I can see that it's an expensive card with a glossy picture on the front, a photograph of flowers on a dark background. As he reads, I picture a woman standing halfway into a kitchen doorway—of course I picture my own kitchen doorway—just coming from the mailbox, a couple of pieces of junk mail in one hand, reading this card, imagining the man's open, reddish face. When the man is done, I say, "She'll always remember where she was when she read that, what she was wearing—" and then feel that I am being sentimental and odd, that I should shut up.

The men take turns reading aloud, moving around the room in order. The man called Stanfield has written about a hawk he sees from his room every night, sitting on the fence, spreading its wings just before there's a scream from the creature it catches. The man sitting next to me won't read what he's written. "But you wrote the most!" I say. He laughs and shakes his head, pleased that I'd noticed, and the others laugh at him.

The next man has written down a memory from childhood, a memory of a fight between his parents, of trying to stay out of their way. I try to tell him I like it, but he doesn't believe me.

The last man to read is Billy. One of Billy's eyes wanders, and there is too much white in that eye, but the other looks gently at me. His piece is about coming out of a pool hall late at night, in the rain. Billy writes that he was standing in the street when a car drove up. A man got out and opened the trunk. "I saw what was inside," Billy reads. The man had a shotgun. Then he shot, and there was blood all over. The man looked at Billy.

"Well," said the man.

"Well," said Billy. Billy walked away.

When he has finished reading, Billy tells the story again, in almost the same words, as if he can't believe that the people in the room can have learned it already from his writing.

.

It's still light outside and still hot when the librarian and I come out of the library and walk past the flower beds. When we have walked half the distance back to the building where I first entered, men start to come out of that building in twos and threes. I can see them clearly in the early twilight, on the other side of the wide yard. The men walk along a concrete path, first at a right angle to the one on which the librarian and I are walking. Then the first men reach the intersection of the paths and turn to come toward the librarian and me, while others are still coming out of the building. Because everyone walks on the concrete paths, not on the grass—taking no shortcuts—and because the men are dressed alike, it looks like a procession, a long column moving closer and closer.

"The A.A. meeting is letting out," says the librarian. "I'm glad it's over. When it's still going on, it's hard to walk through the auditorium with so many people looking at you." There must be two hundred men coming. They are coming toward the librarian and me, and then we are among them. The librarian crosses over to my right so he and not I will have to step off the concrete path—for the men don't give way to us, though they don't take up quite all the room, either. I'm able to stay on the path. The librarian and I walk through the crowd that's going the other way, and that's what I dream of that night, of passing through crowds of men.

WHOM

DID YOU

KILL?

The poetry project at the prison is being filmed. Filmmakers, on a small grant, have flown in from Maryland—but just for the day, so everyone is doing everything at once to give them something to film. Two prisoners are arguing about the layout of *Walls*, the poetry project's magazine. The next issue is spread out on a big table in the corner of the prison schoolroom. The inmate poetry workshop, which usually meets on Tuesdays, is meeting today, though it is Friday. It meets in a small room adjoining the schoolroom, with the men sitting cross-legged on the floor. And the three poetry judges (local people who help out now and then) are sitting in a windowless office on the *other* side of the schoolroom, reading poems by thirty-nine prisoners from all over the country, selecting for the issue after next. The project has been going for two years now, and the poems keep coming in.

The three judges have never before worked together. Usually they stop by separately on some convenient day and look over the poems in the folder. "Are you done with this batch?" they ask one another now, passing piles of poems around. "Top one is—let's see—O'Connell?"

Meanwhile it is an ordinary day at the prison school, where inmates may take math and English courses, and where the poetry project borrows space. Margaret, the older of the two women judges, has trouble concentrating on the poems (some in handwriting, some badly typed) while a grammar lesson takes place on the other side of the wall. "*Whom* did I kill? I killed *him*," says the teacher's voice. She has met the teacher, whose name is Mr. Pratt. She asks herself whether he could have said what she thought she heard.

One of the filmmakers comes into the cubicle and stands behind her, aiming his video camera over her shoulder. She can't help smiling, and meets the eye of the man judge, Steve, who is an English teacher at the community college. The youngest judge, a graduate student, looks *more* serious now that she is being filmed—like a judge. She makes a note on her pad, turning over a page from the sheaf of poems in front of her.

The camera whirs behind Margaret and she looks down at the poem.

> *In my dream, I hear your voice*
> *But it is only a bird. . . .*

She tries to look natural, wondering what she usually does with her arms when she reads poetry. She has been here in this prison several times, reading poems just this way, sometimes in this room, but usually she has been left to herself. One of the prisoners might bring her a cup of coffee, or the head of the poetry project, a prisoner named Wally, has sometimes stopped by to chat. Once, someone she didn't know came in and asked if she'd mail a letter for him. She agreed, not knowing whether she was breaking a rule.

"Is Wally Thornhill *our* Wally?" asks Steve.

"Yes," says Margaret. Most of the poetry submitted to the magazine comes from distant prisons, but the prisoners here, who write poems in their workshop, may also submit poems to the competition they run, though few of them do. They print the magazine, putting elaborate borders and curlicues around the poems, but writing is new to them. Wally has been working hard, though, and the last time Margaret was here, he said he planned to put some poems into the folder. She's glad he's done it. She likes Wally, who seems excruciatingly young to her.

"I'm afraid they're not so good," says Steve.

Margaret hasn't seen the poems yet, but she's upset anyway. "He knows that," she says, not sure it is true. "He's mature about it. He knows he's a beginner. I think it's great that he entered. *That's* the achievement for him."

"Of course," says Steve. He looks hurt, and Margaret is sorry she spoke so quickly. Probably Steve is the gentlest of critics and teachers.

"Wally's interesting," she says apologetically. "He wrote me a thank-you note when I led a workshop here, and I wrote back to say I'd enjoyed doing it. And do you know what? *He* wrote back to *me* to thank me for writing back to him!"

Steve laughs. "You could go on forever," says Ann, the

graduate student. She says it a little severely, as if she thinks it would be a waste of time to go on forever.

"He wrote about seeing my little square envelope with handwriting on it and then catching sight of his name," Margaret says. "I don't think he gets many letters."

They all dip their heads back to the piles of poems. Often Margaret loses heart when she reads here—and then the last few poems may be beautiful. She has always found *something*.

The three judges finish their task at about the same time, and decide it would be all right to talk over their choices. On the whole, they agree, to Margaret's relief. She has never met the other judges, and she isn't sure she likes them; at the same time, she has to admit to herself that she feels easier here this time, not being the only person around (besides the teachers in the schoolroom) who isn't a prisoner.

Now she gathers up the list—the other two judges seem to be letting her lead the way—and the poems, and stuffs everything back into the manila folder, and the three of them leave together, walking quietly through the schoolroom, where the lesson is just ending, and stopping at a desk where one of the teachers is sitting. He offers to escort them outside, and they are about to go, but meanwhile Margaret has spotted Wally through a glass panel in the door of the room where the poetry workshop is still in progress. He is sitting on the floor with the rest of the men. She waves to him, just to be friendly, but he jumps up and comes out, closing the door softly behind him.

By now it is crowded where they are standing. The leader of the filmmakers, a tall black man who someone had said is an ex-convict himself, is leaning over the desk consulting a chart, his back to the others.

"I didn't mean to take you out of the group," Margaret says to Wally. "I was just saying good-bye. But we're done—we left a list in the folder."

"It's a good bunch this time, isn't it?" Wally says. He is not very tall, not much taller than Margaret, and slight. He is black.

"Yes. We loved Perry Mather's work. Did you read those?" The prison authorities insist that outsiders judge the poems, but the prisoners themselves always have favorites, too, and in the end, the decisions are often compromises. The outsiders—Margaret at least—aren't comfortable telling the prisoners what to do.

"The ones about sex in prison?" Wally says, surprised. "You like those?" He smiles. "Yeah, those are cool."

"The long one is really something," says Steve.

"Will they let you print it?" Ann asks. "Four-letter words?"

"I don't know," says Wally. "But what did you think of *my* poems?"

Just then, however, the filmmaker turns around. "Hey," he says, "this is *real*." He gestures to take in the three judges and Wally.

"We're just saying good-bye," says Margaret.

"Well, can we film you saying good-bye, then? This is *real*," he says again.

She laughs and shrugs and the others smile. "OK."

"Can you all wait for a few moments?" he says. "We have to do it in there." He points toward the room where the workshop is still going on.

"You want us to wait until that room is empty so we can go in there just to say good-bye to Wally on videotape?" Ann says.

"If you don't mind," says the man.

Wally goes back to the workshop, and the judges wait, sitting in the schoolroom, which is empty now. Margaret is still holding the folder of poems, and she straightens the contents a few times. It's almost time for the count, when the men have to return to their cells, and then the count is announced on the loudspeakers and uniformed guards appear. Margaret hasn't seen the guards come through the door—they are just suddenly there. The men file out of the room where the workshop has been held and leave the schoolroom, all but Wally, who has been given permission to stay and be filmed saying good-bye. The men wear uniforms—most khaki, a few navy blue. Seen one at a time, they look like people who happen to be dressed in clothes of that color, but seen in a group, they are in uniform.

"You know, I've never known what Wally's in for," Margaret says, almost to herself, as the group files past them and out of the schoolroom.

"Manslaughter," says Ann. "But they all consider themselves political prisoners, you know."

Margaret doesn't answer. She has never been sure about the difference between manslaughter and murder. She cannot imagine Wally killing someone in any way, by accident or on purpose. She would like to think that Ann is mistaken, that Wally stole cars, but Ann doesn't seem like the sort of person who is mistaken. She wonders how Ann knows.

In the small room where the camera is set up, the filmmakers now seat them in folding chairs: Steve, Ann, and

Margaret in a row, and Wally opposite them. It feels like
an arrangement of chairs that would never have happened
to happen on its own.

"Now, if you could just talk the way you did before, and
maybe about the poems and so forth," says the chief filmmaker. The camera is turned on. Margaret looks at Wally
and he smiles.

"Thank you all for coming in and reading these poems,"
he says, only a little stiffly.

Margaret thinks that if he can be a good sport, so can
she. "We enjoyed it," she says. She finally hands him the
folder. "There are some good ones. Did you read Perry
Mather's? The man from Texas?"

"Yes, he's very good," says Wally.

Ann says, "His poems seem nicely grounded in sensory
detail." Then her voice grows younger. "I kind of liked
that."

Wally looks over at her eagerly. Margaret wonders
whether he knows what she means, and also whether Ann
is joking—the poems are impressive, but, after all, possibly obscene—and whether Wally thinks Ann is joking.
What makes him seem young is his forehead, she decides—it is smooth and broad and black, giving his eyes,
which are set far apart, a particular look of surprise and
trust. He is not as young as she thought. He is probably
twenty-five. Margaret is forty, just old enough, she has
realized lately, to be the mother of an adult, if she had
had children early, which she didn't; her two children are
not yet in school. Wally is not young enough to be her
son. He is almost old enough to be her younger brother.

"I wanted to ask you what you thought of *my* poems,"
Wally says now, looking at each of them, and he seems

completely natural. Whatever else this occasion is, it is also the one time they have ever just sat and talked like friends, and probably it will never happen again. He won't be at this prison much longer. The last time Margaret was here, one of the teachers told her that Wally had been sentenced and was going to be sent somewhere else. The day they talked, she hadn't wanted to ask what his crime was or how long he would be in prison.

Steve and Ann do not answer Wally's question, but Margaret is so certain that Wally knows he is a beginner, she just blurts it out. "I think it's *great* that you entered," she says. "Of course, you have a lot to learn. You're just getting started."

"So they're no good?" he asks, and he looks disappointed. He looks like a man who's been sentenced, as if, somehow, what she has said is as bad as what the judge said—the real judge.

"No," she says quickly. "Actually, I liked one of them a lot. The one about your father." She no longer knows whether she is telling the truth, but she thinks she still may be. Most of Wally's poems were totally vague—meaningless—but the one about his father was a simple, straightforward narrative, even a touching narrative.

"Yes, that's a good one," Wally says.

"I liked it, too," says Steve, and Margaret sees that he is trying to straighten things out.

"You say what happened very simply. . . ." Margaret begins, but she can't think of anything more to say. The poem was sad, a memory of unjust childhood punishment, of cruelty, really.

"Speaking of sensory detail," says Ann now, and she

sounds like someone in a graduate seminar, "that's what's so good about this poem. That's why it works."

"Right," Steve breaks in. "Detail. You know, Wally— you *can* write very well, with lots of detail. That's what it takes. Margaret was telling us about your letter to her— how you were glad she wrote to you. And you talked about catching sight of your name on her envelope. Now that's so much more *interesting* than if you'd just said it was nice to hear from her."

Wally sits up straighter in his chair. Margaret is saying, "Look, Wally—" but she can't imagine how to explain.

"A letter means a lot to us here," Wally says.

"I know!" says Steve.

Margaret wants to grab Wally and pull him out of the room, to say something, to say, "You're worth ten of them." And yet she knows it probably isn't true. In a sense she doesn't actually know him. In a way, she knows Ann and Steve, whom she has just met, better—she knows what books are on their shelves, who their friends and relatives are, what movies they like.

Soon the filming is over, and a guard comes to take Wally back to his cell and also to escort the three poetry judges to the exit. As they leave the schoolroom, Wally turns to Margaret and says, "May I ask you something?"

"Of course." To her surprise, everyone waits—the guard, everyone—and they step away from the others.

"Was it wrong that I wrote to you?" Wally asks her.

She has been given a second chance. "No," she says emphatically. "No. I loved it that you wrote to me." She touches his arm.

But he looks unsure. They all set out down the corridor

like colleagues in an office building. Wally shakes hands and says good-bye where two corridors meet, and then the guard walks the three poetry judges farther along. They wait and laugh a little, nervously, as the inner electronic door takes its time to open. Then they step into the space between the inner door and the outer door. The guard leaves, and another guard, at the desk, waves through a glass pane as they take off their plastic visitors' badges and stick them through a slot in the wall of his office. Then the outer electronic door slides open, and the three of them step into the waiting room and outside, where they suddenly remember what season it is—spring—and what kind of weather they are having.

A BASKET OF ORANGES

Mr. Cordero brought doughnuts to the joint meeting of the Prison Poetry Society and its advisory committee: several large boxes, assorted, from Dunkin' Donuts—jelly, cream, chocolate, coconut. Actually, the advisory committee was mostly an idea just then, and I think I was the only person present who wasn't an inmate and didn't work in the prison. Mr. Cordero was a teacher there.

We were a dozen people sitting at a long wooden table in a room just large enough for it. I sat in the last chair on one side. At the opposite end of the table, at the head, was James LeRoy, the inmate director of the Poetry Society, who talked fast in a smooth, light, liquid voice and used long words, occasionally incorrectly. On his left was his new assistant, Maurice Hughes, whom I'd never seen before. Maurice had dreadlocks, which I'd never seen up close—the hair was huge and matted. I stared, trying to decide whether hair would get that way if you just neglected it or whether he'd had to work at it. He looked brainy, too. Maurice and James threw big words back and forth and then down the table at me. They'd worked out all sorts of official jobs and positions—coordinator of this for the society, implementer of that for the advisory committee—but I was the committee, and Maurice was a lot of the society: much of the discussion ended with Maurice and me agreeing to do what had to be done, things like investigating cheap paper suppliers for the society's small, occasional poetry magazine. We'd look at each other, kitty-corner down the table, and nod. At some point in all this I understood that Maurice and I were thinking alike—maybe about the exact way in which all of this was funny—but I don't know how I knew.

After a while we stopped discussing and passed the doughnuts around with much hoopla. We ate and licked our fingers and talked. It took a while. Then Maurice looked around the table. "*Are* we sated?" he said. When the meeting broke up and we were all filing out into the corridor, he came over to me. Suddenly he looked *young* (it turned out later we'd each assumed the other was ten years younger, but we were the same age, forty-four) and also like a hood. He looked at me as if he thought I might not look back. "I'll need your phone number."

I gave it to him, of course. Then I went home and found out the information I'd promised to find out and wrote Maurice a letter, but when I got an answer a couple of weeks later, it was from a different prison. He'd been transferred to a minimum security prison fifty miles away. He'd never cared for poetry, he said. The society was just something to do. He couldn't bear James LeRoy. "That isn't his name," he wrote. "He's dangerous." He told me about the new prison: there was a beautiful lake he could see but couldn't get to. I had trouble with his handwriting but I answered the letter and he wrote again. He wasn't boring, and he didn't get angry when I asked questions. (Why do you wear dreadlocks? What are you there for?)

He was a bank robber, but he'd also sold drugs. Not anymore—he wouldn't sell drugs anymore. He was a Rastafarian and he didn't eat meat. "Don't give your kids processed foods," he'd plead with me at the end of each letter. *"Don't eat meat."* I wrote him that I'd started driving again. I'd been afraid and hadn't driven for years. Now my husband's stepfather had died, and we'd inherited his car: a big white Buick that had to be sent from Florida on a long truck that carried two layers of cars on metal tracks. The truck filled our whole block when it showed up. The new car had an automatic transmission—we'd always had small foreign cars with standard shift, and I'd never tried an automatic. I could drive it. It was so big I felt safe, though my friends laughed at me for driving a huge white Buick. When I drove it, I would hear Abe, my husband's dead stepfather, talking to me. He was old and blunt and very Jewish. He saw no reason why I shouldn't drive.

"But be careful," wrote Maurice.

We wrote to each other for a year. Once he had a weekend furlough and he said he'd come see me. He'd be in our city, New Haven, on a Saturday. He loved popcorn, he said. A friend had given our children a popcorn maker, so I wrote him that my kids would fix popcorn for him.

"You'll let me come to your house?" he wrote. "You aren't afraid I'll steal your silver and china?"

I wrote back, "All I have worth stealing is this type-writer."

"I don't rob *typewriters*," Maurice flung back at me in the next letter, a few days later. "I rob *banks*."

But he wasn't coming, he wrote at the last minute. He'd been put in touch with a woman and he was spending his furlough with her. He predicted he'd regret it, and he did. And then he was released—maybe a month later—and after the last letter from prison saying, "I'll call you in a few days," there was nothing.

Months later—maybe four months—the phone rang one morning and it was Maurice. He'd be in New Haven that day, he said. He'd be visiting his aunt. He was coming by bus from New York, where he was living. "I'll pick you up," I said. He told me where his aunt lived, and I said I'd be there at two o'clock.

I had to look up the street on a map. It wasn't far, though; it was off a street I knew how to reach. I could drive there.

I was not actually frightened when I drove in those days; in fact, I enjoyed it. But it was a *thing*, never quite offhand. Knowing that I'd have to drive later was like knowing I'd be expected to answer a difficult question: I'd rehearse in my mind; I'd prefer that it not be postponed. Driving itself mattered more than almost anything I might be driving *to*. After driving, I was proud of myself, but a little used up. I'd need sweet tea or a cookie.

It was a clear, cold windy day in March. I thought through the route to Maurice's aunt's house street by street, planning two turns ahead of what I was doing. I turned right into his aunt's street and pulled into the first available parking space. Around me were empty lots and the remains of a playground. Beyond them was a small brick housing project. Soon Maurice came out of one of the low buildings and came toward me. I remembered him, but of course that was partly because of the dreadlocks.

He opened the passenger door and slid in beside me, turning his face and giving me his cheek to kiss, as if he were much older than I. His cheek was soft and creased, very black. I kissed him and drove farther along the street, looking for a place to turn. The car seemed large, but there was a wide space at the end—it was a dead-end street, with more empty lots around it—and we headed back toward the main thoroughfare and my house.

"My aunt didn't want me to come," he said. "I had to promise I'd call her as soon as I get to your house."

"What did she think I'd do to you?"

He shook his head. "She's afraid of everything. It's dangerous where she lives—she's afraid to go out."

"I didn't see anyone at all."

"Even the little kids sell drugs. If I hadn't gone over to your car you'd have been approached. It's assumed a white person would only come there for one reason."

I pulled up in front of my house. "Shall I lock the door?" he said.

"We usually don't bother. Or—what we really do is, we leave one door unlocked."

"Why do you do that?"

"I don't know," I said. "Abe would have wanted us to lock it, but we never locked our old car. . . ."

He laughed.

"You seem sad," I said, even though he'd just laughed.

"I know."

We went into the house. None of my children was home.

I wondered how the house seemed to him. It's small, with lots of books. In the kitchen are a big table and chairs, wooden cabinets, and a three-tiered set of hanging wire baskets—small, large, and larger—holding red and blue napkins, bananas, oranges, or apples. On that day the top basket held oranges, huge ones I'd bought that weekend, very bright orange. The sun shone into the room.

I made coffee. He phoned his aunt twice. We sat and talked. We didn't run out of topics. Every once in a while he'd turn to the phone and make a call. "Jamal?" he said to one of the people who answered. "What are you doing? Who's with you? Nobody at *all*? Now, you won't go outside, will you?" He hung up. "My son," he said to me.

"I didn't know you had a son!"

"I have seven children," he said. "He's five. He's very smart. He's doomed."

"You have seven children?"

I asked him to come to dinner the next day. My husband and the children would be home. My oldest boy would play the guitar.

"I don't eat meat."

"I know *that*. I wouldn't give you meat."

"I like fish," he said.

"OK. I'll make fish."

"What time shall I come?"

"Six-thirty?"

We agreed that he'd phone at six-thirty and tell us where he was. One of us would pick him up. He stood up. "I need to get back to my aunt."

He stood looking at the basket of oranges. "They're beautiful."

"Yes."

"Won't they dry out?" he said.

"I'll eat them before they can," I said. He looked startled, as if he hadn't thought that they would be eaten.

"Would you like one?"

He shook his head. We went out to the car. I remembered a better route to his aunt's. I steered the car carefully through our narrow streets.

Rounding a corner, I thought about cooking fish. I make it simply. He was a West Indian—it wouldn't be good enough for him, my broiled flounder with lemon, and even if there was a package in the freezer—I wasn't sure—it might not be large enough.

"Do you think you'd like vegetables and spaghetti?" I asked. "I make spaghetti with tomatoes and eggplant. . . ."

"Sure. That would be fine. I like eggplant."

We reached his aunt's corner and I pulled over to let him out. The next day, I cooked the eggplant and it turned out well, but Maurice never called or came, and I have never heard from him again.

THE

GIRAFFES

Maxine and I have been friends for seventeen years. We met in the East Rock Park playground when our daughters were two, and now they are in college. Pushing them on the swings, we'd argue. Maxine said she needed to *know* whether there is another, incorporeal reality. I said I didn't care, I couldn't imagine it anyway. "If I can't eat, I'm not interested," I said. Maxine said the world around us—the mud, the Horsie Swing (which was both girls' favorite but was usually broken), the glider on which they could ride together—all this might be unreal.

Now, quite often, Maxine is alone in her big house when I come to visit. In the old days we often wondered if we'd stay married and have more babies. Eventually I got divorced, and then Maxine did, although not until she had a son. He's now eleven, but he often seems to be at hockey practice or staying overnight at a teammate's house. My house is quiet, too, but the quiet at Maxine's is more noticeable.

On my way home from work I sometimes stop there for a glass of wine or, occasionally, dinner. When I come up on the porch, the house—the same house she and her husband lived in—seems dark and empty, but when I ring the doorbell and look into the glass pane on her front door, I see a line of light way at the back, which is Maxine's office. She's a psychotherapist. Her last client will have left long ago, but she's making notes or working on an article she's writing. She hasn't noticed the darkness because the lamp in her office is always on, and only when she hears the doorbell does she realize how late it is. First, a light comes on in her kitchen, and I see bright yellow walls and ceramic pots on shelves. The dog, an elderly golden retriever, wakes up and hurries toward the front door, shifting from side to side because she's fat and her hips are unsteady. Then comes Maxine, in a long dark skirt and a white sweater. She turns on the next light, smiling because she knows I can see her, and the dark red, old-fashioned wallpaper in the hall appears. It is as if she is conceding that, after all, each room in turn is real.

When I went over to Maxine's a few weeks ago, I resolved, as I stood on the porch, not to go on and on about Randolph. I work for a graphic design firm, and Randolph, a veterinary professor at Tufts who is writing a book about cats, was put in touch with our firm by his publisher. I'd done drawings of animals before, and I'm doing the illustrations and diagrams for Randolph's book. We met for lunch, and it came out that we were both divorced. Then we made a plan to see each other again. Randolph stumbled over his words, laughing, outside the restaurant, as if he'd never invited a woman to dinner before. He said he often drove through New Haven, where I live. "I'm seeing some-one," I told Maxine, though I never go out with men I work with. Sure enough, we made still another date and we started sleeping together. I brought him to my house.

"I was asleep," Maxine said, coming to the door. "I'm sorry it's so dark—the porch light is out."

"I thought you were working."

"I lay down to think and I fell asleep. But I remembered you were coming."

Sometimes she forgets, but this time she'd even cooked vegetable curry and rice in advance. She poured a glass of wine for me. The kitchen was light and inviting, and the food smelled good. I didn't offer to help, I just sat there feeling happy. We ate, and then we sat before our empty plates, talking for a long time. "It's different from when the children were little," I said. I'd been noticing that we sometimes paused before speaking. We weren't always struggling to keep to a subject, fighting interruptions.

"Alex is still little in a way," she said. "But he'll be eleven this week."

"Not so little."

"We're going to the Bronx Zoo to celebrate on Saturday," she said.

"You and a crowd of eleven-year-olds?"

"Just one other kid."

"Do you want me to come?" I said. It was May, and I had a vision of quiet paths at the zoo—filled with people, of course, but peaceful anyhow—and animals serenely watching from meadows and fields.

"You'd come?" said Maxine.

"We'd have hours to talk." I love to look at animals. Then I wondered whether the daughters might like to come, too. Mine, Rosalind, was coming home from college the next day, and Jessica, Maxine's daughter, the day after that.

"Jessica doesn't approve of zoos," said Maxine. She was standing up. "I want to show you something," she said. She is tall and fair, and she always has a slight frown, not as if she disapproves, but as if she is listening attentively. I find myself thinking she will have what she wants, maybe because she is long-waisted and has a long, graceful neck. I am short-waisted, with no neck to speak of, and somehow I imagine that long-waisted women get what they like, as if they are able to lean over farther than the rest of us to reach it.

Maxine brought in a photograph that had been clipped from the newspaper—a man handing something to a man and a woman, all of them smiling. "Do you know Frank Parks?" she said.

"No."

"He's the man taking the check. He's the chairman of the board of a ballet school for poor kids."

"What about him?"

"He lives in this neighborhood," she said. "He runs past my house. I've been seeing him for years and I never knew who he was until one day he turned his ankle and sat down on my steps. I went out and talked to him. I offered to drive him home."

She was still standing, holding the photograph by one corner. "And now, suddenly, we have a very high coincidence rate. I bet he's never been in the paper before, and I hardly ever get past the first page. The other day, something made me read it—and there's Frank. I've met him four or five times. I was at the Yale Rep and there he was with his wife, two rows in front of me. Now we talk and know names. We have conversations about how we didn't meet all these years."

"You're thinking about him."

"Yes. I'm always talking to him in my mind. Did you ever do that—sort of mentally explain your life to a new man?"

I nodded. When Maxine had gone to get the picture, I'd been describing her in my mind to Randolph.

"He might be thinking about me, too," she said. "I can't tell." She put the kettle on for tea.

"Is this a good idea?" I asked.

"Why not?"

"He's married," I said. "Pain, pain, pain."

When the tea was ready she sat down with hers and handed me mine. "Not if I just think," she said. She always forgets I take sugar, and I stood up to get it.

"You're not going to just think forever."

"I might," she said. "I don't want to have an affair—I'm too busy."

"Then what's the point of the thinking?"

"I like thinking," she said. "Daydreaming, I guess. You do, too."

"But Randolph is real."

She had stood up again and opened a package of

cookies—good, expensive ones—and put some on a plate. "You're right," she said suddenly. "Randolph is real. Frank is imaginary, more or less. That's not good." I took a cookie. "The girls aren't like this," she said. "Rosalind and Jessica do not fall in love with imaginary guys. And besides, I'm forty-six."

"It's not so bad," I said, thinking I'd upset her.

"In a way, it *is* real," said Maxine.

.

The next day, Wednesday, Rosalind came home from college and sure enough, she was not in love with anybody imaginary. She was calm and cheerful, tired from exams. I didn't mention Randolph the first night. On Thursday I called to tell him some drawings were complete. "That's wonderful," he said. "Look, why don't you bring them to my house tonight?"

"All the way to Boston?"

"Well, I'd love to see them," he said. "We could get something to eat, and then later some of my colleagues are coming over. I'm sure they'd like to see the drawings, too." It's a two-and-a-half-hour drive to Boston, but I agreed.

"What colleagues?" said Rosalind when I saw her at home just before I left. I was changing my clothes.

"He's a professor in the veterinary school at Tufts," I said. "Maybe these are other professors."

"Do you want me to come with you?" said Rosalind.

"Why?"

"I don't know. It sounds funny to me."

"Actually, I'm involved with this guy," I said.

"I assumed," she said. "But the drawings of cats . . . well, I don't know."

I looked at a map. "Have a nice supper," she said as I left, as if she were my mother.

I rode with my drawings between stiff boards beside me on the front seat of the car. I found Randolph's house in Watertown without any trouble. I always expect divorced men to live in apartments, but this was a small house with a two-step porch in front. A long wooden ramp with a handrail ran straight up the walk and onto the steps, like the gangplank of a ship. I was tempted to walk up it, but I didn't because it belonged to someone else—although to whom I couldn't imagine. I knew Randolph had children who sometimes stayed with him, but he hadn't said any of them used a wheelchair.

The ramp took up all the space in front of the door. When I reached the top, I had to hop onto it to ring the bell, but then the importance of seeing Randolph made me forget the ramp. I'd been imagining him so much that his real presence, when the door opened, was a kind of metaphysical joke. His hair was grayer than it had been in my thoughts, but his smile was young.

Randolph took my coat and kissed me. He led me into the living room and lit a lamp, although there was already a light on. I was hungry, but we didn't seem to be going out to dinner yet. He hung my coat in a closet.

The living room was also Randolph's study. It had a desk at one end, but piles of paper had traveled off it onto the sofa, and a cat lay on top of them. I sat next to the cat, and a dog presented himself to be petted. Whenever I took my hand away, he quietly thrust his head under it again. He had smooth black hair and smooth hanging ears, as if years of petting had flattened them and also tamed him; he was a soulful dog.

Randolph looked at me with happy amusement. He seemed to think it was charming but odd of me to be sitting there petting his dog. He's fifty, but if everyone has a Real Permanent Age, his is fourteen, and from the first I had liked his look of freshness, which seemed to say that nothing that was happening had ever happened before. The first time we went to bed, he was as alert and delighted as if the sexual act had been described to him beforehand, but he hadn't really believed that men and women do such things.

"Well, there have been *some* women, of course. . . ." he'd said, the one time we'd talked about our lives since our divorces.

Randolph lit still another lamp and undid my package of drawings reverently, holding it well away from the dog. He looked at each one carefully and laughed often, though none of them was funny, and made many comments and suggestions. Then he began showing me pages from his book and places where he'd just decided that additional illustrations or diagrams might be useful.

"These cats you drew are full of their organs," he said. "That's good, Valerie. We don't want roomy-looking cats." He glanced at the cat on the sofa, who did look roomy— with that loose skin that makes an extra fold when a cat lies down. He hadn't moved, even when the dog came close. I tried to imagine his organs.

After a while Randolph offered me tea. I was surprised— tea didn't seem like a prelude to dinner—and I said I was hungry, but Randolph only said, "Oh . . . I don't have much around," and went into the kitchen. "So what kind of tea do you like?" he called after a few minutes. "Cranberry Cove? Wild Forest Blackberry? Or do you like tea-type tea?"

"Anything. Lipton's. Not herbal."

"Some of the herbal ones aren't bad," he said cheerfully when he came in with my brown tea and his red tea.

I'd have happily postponed dinner indefinitely if we were going to bed, and that was what I thought was going on at first. But I kept sitting there while periodically the dog would remember he hadn't been petted enough, and Randolph kept bringing in more unconnected paragraphs from his book. He seemed to keep pieces of it in every room of his house. He kept rushing past me in different directions.

I had just made up my mind to forget about bed and ask if I could fix myself an egg when the doorbell rang, and I remembered the colleagues. I stood up and followed Randolph to the door. When he opened it, on the lit porch was a smiling woman seated in air. Her knees were bent, that is, as if she were in a chair, but there was no chair under her. Her left arm was hooked firmly over the ramp's handrail, and her right arm was grasping her left arm. "Have you been waxing your ramp, or what?" she said.

"Where's your chair?" said Randolph.

"Down there." She gestured with her chin. After a second's delay, Randolph and I made sense of it at the same time, and he leaned down and put his arms under the woman's body while I squeezed past him and ran down the walk. A few feet from the bottom of the ramp was an empty wheelchair. I pushed it up quickly and the woman, who had been saying, "I'm not falling—it's all right," lowered herself into it. I started to push it into the house, but she reached for the wheels and spun away from me into the hall, where she turned the chair around and faced us. She had rumpled thick brown hair and bangs. She was younger than I am. "I don't usually make such a dramatic entrance," she said.

Randolph said she was his colleague, Andrea McGuire, and we shook hands, and then Andrea wheeled herself into the living room, where the dog jumped onto the sofa to lick her face. "Hi, Chester," she said. She took off her jacket and tossed it onto a chair. It was a boyish, bright-blue jacket. Without it she was thin, and I was surprised that she'd been able to hold herself up on the railing.

"Are you all right?" I said. "Are you hurt?"

"It was kind of fun," said Andrea. "My arms are pretty strong from wheeling the chair, and I work out."

"Actually, you looked wonderful, hanging there," Randolph said. "How did it happen?"

"I guess I leaned too far forward to ring the bell," said Andrea. "I wasn't high enough on the ramp. First the chair started to slip away, so I grabbed the railing, which pulled me up a bit, and then it really did slip away."

The doorbell rang again. This time it was a man named Murray, who entered without incident, walking on his feet, which somehow made Randolph and Andrea—and then me, too—laugh, and Murray's eyebrows went up; and so Andrea's arrival had to be described to Murray, who was more interested in Randolph's book. He'd seen a copy of the manuscript. He was not especially interested in my drawings, but Andrea looked at them politely. I had kept my now empty teacup, and after a while Andrea said, "I want tea. Do you want some more, Valerie?"

"No, thanks," I said, and watched from the sofa how she spun familiarly around a lamp table that was near the doorway, wheeled herself down the hall, then reached up with her left hand at exactly the right spot to flick the switch and turn on the light in the kitchen—which finally made me know what I must have known, in some way, all along, because of the ramp: she was Randolph's lover.

I know how a woman looks in the house where she lives and I knew Andrea didn't live there, but came often, stayed overnight and kept a few clothes there. I gathered my drawings and left soon after that, and cried in the car in the dark. Randolph had walked me to the door. "I'm sorry," he said. It was as if he had handed me a message when he couldn't tell me something. I stopped at a pancake house on my way home. I wanted something filling and sweet.

.

At the last minute Jessica and Rosalind decided to come to the zoo with us. Jessica did disapprove, but she said it was important to know what went on at zoos, *particularly* if one disapproved. Rosalind thought some zoos were less distressing than others, and she said it would be fun to go to the Bronx Zoo. She said we'd last been there when she was five, and I'd insisted on leaving early—she claimed she'd wanted to get back ever since. Usually when she comes home there is a week or so of little starts of pleasure before I get used to her again, but this time I was too upset about Randolph to be delighted. Still, I was glad the girls were coming. We'd have to take two cars, and they said they'd drive Maxine's car while Maxine and the two boys and I took mine.

So I drove to Maxine's house on Saturday morning. It was a chilly, sunny day. When I drew up to the curb, Maxine was standing on a ladder on her porch, leaning forward against it almost luxuriously, her arm curved upward so that she could screw in the new light bulb. "I finally remembered to do this," she called. The curve of her arm was so lovely that for an instant it took away the sharp ache I'd felt since Thursday night. For that moment I thought I could manage, just looking at what's beautiful, but then her arm reminded me of something and I identified it as Andrea's arm, curled magically around the handrail.

Rosalind got out of my car and Maxine came down the ladder and went for the boys and a jacket. Alex and his friend, Geoffrey, put the ladder away and then we left. As we drove off, I saw Jessica come out onto the porch and she and Rosalind, two big young women in T-shirts ("It's May, Mom," Rosalind had said when I put on a heavy sweater) hugged like toddlers, with their whole selves pressed together.

For a while Maxine and I were silent while the boys in the back seat chattered. Then she said, "I had a long talk with Frank."

"No kidding," I said. "Was it good?"

"Great," she said. "I'm scared, though."

"How did it happen?"

"I made it happen," said Maxine. "I went running when I knew he'd come along." Her voice was rich and happy.

"Watch out," I said.

"You think I'm looking for trouble?"

"Oh, don't ask me," I said. "I'm such an idiot."

"What's wrong?" She turned in her seat to face me, within her shoulder harness, and I told her about Thursday night—how Randolph had asked me to bring the drawings, how I thought it was an excuse to go to bed, how he never even fed me dinner.

"You drove to Boston and never got *dinner*?"

"That's right."

I didn't say anything more for a while—I was concentrating on the road—but then I said, "And then his girlfriend showed up."

"He has a girlfriend?"

"So it seems."

"How could you tell?"

"She asked me if I wanted more tea," I said.

Maxine laughed. I told her about the ramp and the wheelchair, but then Alex asked her a question and that was the end of the conversation.

Geoffrey had said he went to the zoo with his family all the time, and the place to meet was the Bronxdale Parking Lot. Jessica and Rosalind arrived there just before we did, and we saw them sitting in the grass in their T-shirts, waving at us, when we drove in. At the zoo entrance, we were handed a map and Geoffrey took it. Ordinarily I'd have wanted it—I like to know where I'm going—but I was feeling sad and *little*, in a way; if this eleven-year-old wanted to be in charge, so be it.

"First, let's go to the World of Birds," Geoffrey said promptly. Off we went, and Geoffrey and Alex told us which way to turn when we came to a crossroads. I was thinking about the times in the coming months when I'd have to talk to Randolph about drawings.

"It's so odd," Maxine said as we walked. "Do you think he *forgot* he said dinner? Did he eat before you came?"

"I don't know," I said. "I don't think he forgot." I had that dark feeling when you want to *be* in darkness, and then we reached the World of Birds, and it was dark: dark halls with large, brightly lit scraps of jungle next to us, like the huge dioramas in a natural history museum, but with live birds. We looked at the identifying drawings and spotted bright birds scattered in the trees or saw them fly, but it was hard to believe they were real. My favorite scene was the most familiar one, with birds I saw or tried to find near home. There was a summer tanager, a red bird. "I guess he's wicked," I said quietly now to Maxine.

"Who's wicked—Randolph?" said Rosalind, overhearing me. "I *told* you I should have gone with you." She'd listened sympathetically Thursday night and agreed that Andrea was probably Randolph's lover. "Men and women can just be friends," she said. "But it would have had a different feel. And you would have gotten dinner."

Maxine said now, "He may have simply enjoyed seeing you together. His women."

"Some guys get off on that," said Jessica. Rosalind must have told her the story. I dropped back to see the tanager again, though it didn't interest me as much as if I'd spotted one in the park, and the others got ahead of me, but Maxine waited for me to catch up. We stepped out into the sun again. Geoffrey and Alex were looking over the map, impatient to move on.

"But I liked Andrea," I said. I'd been aware since we arrived of wheelchairs—we'd seen two people using them—and the ways in which the zoo would be convenient or inconvenient if you were on wheels. I'd been imagining Andrea at the zoo. The thought of her, in fact, cheered me up, and I realized I was quite hungry.

"He's cheating on Andrea," Maxine said.

"Right," I said. "I'm angry with him on her behalf, as if I knew her. As if he were cheating on you."

Now Geoffrey interrupted to announce that the next place we'd go would be the World of Darkness.

I turned to him. "You're awfully fond of these *worlds* they have here," I said. He blinked several times and looked at me as if he'd just noticed me. "You'll like it," he said. He was a thin blond kid with a sharp nose.

"But what about lunch?" I said. I'd had enough darkness.

"There's a snack bar near the World of Darkness," said Geoffrey. "My father and I had nachos there."

"I don't want nachos, I want a decent lunch," I said. I made him give me the map. It took a while to figure out where we were and where the food was. Then I said, "Look, we'll take the cable car that goes up in the air. You'll like that, and it comes down near the cafeteria."

"Oh, the Skyfari, sure," said Geoffrey. He and Alex liked anything that smart human beings had been fooling with; I preferred scrubby bushes and strange striped deer gliding through them.

The girls said they'd walk to the cafeteria, but the rest of us took the cable cars. I liked the ride, actually, as much as the kids did. I spotted a herd of giraffes, just like giraffes in pictures, and I said we had to get back and see them close up. Maxine was less interested. She kept asking me questions about Randolph and Andrea.

Jessica and Rosalind came puffing along while we were eating lunch and went off to buy food for themselves and a dish of fruit for me. I'd had a sandwich but I wanted more.

"You're still hungry from Thursday night," Maxine said, as I ate the fruit.

"It did make me extremely hungry!" I said. I was laughing now, but Rosalind said, "Mom, I just can't understand women of your generation. You get so carried away—"

"Yes, but it's so interesting," I said quickly. For the moment, I'd stepped back from the pain. It was like the teeth of a wild beast viewed through a fence, and I saw how the episode would look once I got over it. This was only a temporary respite, but eventually Randolph would be just a story—the man who made me come to Boston but didn't feed me dinner. "All right," I said. "So you girls don't daydream all day long about undeserving men. But what I want to know is—how is that possible?"

Jessica and Rosalind laughed and looked at each other. Jessica's chubby, not built like her mother, but with the same blond hair. She's majoring in chemistry, thinking of medical school. "Well, we do suffer," she said. "We do suffer over men."

We all got up then and went to watch the sea lions, and then Geoffrey steered us toward the monorail—Wild Asia, it was called. I wanted to see those giraffes I'd glimpsed from the sky, and we hadn't yet seen lions. The animals Geoffrey kept showing me, in their carefully designed habitats (by now he was following me, asking me whether I wasn't impressed), were not startling enough for me. I seized the map and agreed on Wild Asia (Maxine and the girls didn't seem to care) as long as we took a route that passed both the giraffes and the lions. But I'd misread the map, we didn't pass them, and Geoffrey wouldn't detour.

"We planned on Wild Asia," he said.

"All right," I said, being nicer than I felt. "Wild Asia. But then giraffes and lions."

At Wild Asia there was a train of little cars that passed through jungles and forests while the voice of a young woman told us what to look at. We crossed a gray New York river. "Imagination is critical!" said the young woman. "This is the Ganges"—and then a calm, heavy tiger padded quietly into the water.

Geoffrey and Alex and the girls never did see the lions or the giraffes. After Wild Asia, they all flopped down on a bench and said they were tired, but Maxine studied the map and the two of us set out. "How could we go to the zoo and not see the lions, anyway?" I asked her.

"Inconceivable."

We saw only one lion. He was lying down, quiet and undramatic, at a distance from us, but he looked so natural in the ordinary New York parkland that I jumped when I noticed him. He was stretched out like a cat, and I imagined his organs, like the cat's, stacked and arrayed inside him. I knew why people got killed sneaking into enclosures like his—I wanted to touch him.

We watched him do nothing for a long time, and I thought about Randolph. "I was a fool," I said. "I was living in a make-believe world."

"Imagination is critical," said Maxine, holding up one finger. "But I know. All the dialogue we think up that will never be said. All the scenes that will never happen. Do the girls really live without that?"

"I feel awful," I said. I had passed through the moment of distance and I was depressed again, because I was tired, I suppose.

"It's not just you, Val," she said. "I've fallen for a hundred guys. Frank is number one hundred."

"Have you ever fallen for one named Randolph?"

"Randolph," said Maxine, smiling. "I don't think so. I

recall a Tom, two Kens . . . I don't remember a Randolph.
What's his last name?"

I'd never mentioned it. "Beekman."

"Randolph Beekman," she said. "Oh, my God. *Randy
Beekman.* Yes, in answer to your question."

She'd gone bright red and had stopped and turned to
face me there on the cobblestone zoo path.

"You've fallen for *Randolph?*" I said.

"Randy Beekman. I knew him at Cornell. Tall? Reddish
hair? Looks like a kid?"

"Yes."

She put her arm around me. "Oh, Valerie, he's hand-
some and funny. He cares about animals. Anybody could
fall for him."

"So why didn't you marry him or something?"

"One afternoon I dropped in to see him," she said. "I
knocked on the door of his dorm room, and he said, 'Come
in' and there was a girl in bed with him."

"Oh, Maxine!"

"It's funny now. But I can see how you might not get
fed by Randy Beekman. He's not actually wicked, I don't
think. But he's certainly not *good.*"

Then she said, "It's funny, I pictured somebody with a
different look."

We walked with our arms around each other for a few
steps and then stopped doing that, for unlike our children
we're never entirely without self-consciousness. We didn't
talk much about the coincidence. I wasn't as surprised as
I might have been, just grateful, as if I'd lost a button I'd
liked from my shirt, and Maxine had reached into her
handbag and pulled out one that matched. But there were

the giraffes at last, seven of them, and ostriches mixed in with them, as if they all belonged to a Tall Animals' Club. The giraffes were *not* the way I'd imagined them, not like pictures or stuffed giraffes, not the way they'd seemed from the air. They walked with a slight forward bend to their knees, a little dip. First the two left legs would take a step, then the two right. Their heads and necks leaned forward—there was a continuous slope down from head to back to rump: one line, one rather lovely line. Their heads dipped rhythmically.

I watched one. His skin was like the shell of a turtle, with squamous brown shapes that had rivers of gold between them. He had two short horns. His ears lay back and he had wide, low eyes, with eyelids, knowing eyes, eyes full of seeing, inner and outer. He looked to me as if he felt utter calm—though surely calm's opposite, fear, was built into his body. It seemed to me that he thought about everything, everything that was or could be, but did not wish for it.

A

WINDING

STAIR

Alan wanted to be loved, unlike some people. He was freckled and fair, and Marsha, who was brown-haired, was beguiled by his coloring. Now she stretched her arm out and ruffled his eyebrow as he got out of her bed. "It's attached," he said. He was not good-looking.

She had known Alan before she met Tom, early in 1973, and during the time she went with Tom she'd occasionally hear from Alan. "Let's walk," Tom would say, all that year. Marsha would be light-limbed and a little sore after sex. They'd dress, she in two sweaters under her coat, and walk through the dark, cold Cambridge streets for hours, saying almost nothing. Tom wore sweaters, too (often without a coat), and sometimes a wool-clad arm would circle her shoulders, but mostly they walked without touching, Marsha keeping her bag on the arm away from Tom in case he wanted to hold hands with her. They were both graduate students at Harvard, and Marsha was a teaching fellow there.

Sometimes when she got home her roommate—she had a roommate then—would tell her Alan had called. Once he sent her a postcard, cheerful and brief. Alan lived in New Haven—he was a student in the school of architecture at Yale. He wanted to fix up slums, he told her, not to build skyscrapers. When she visited him these days they often toured the Hill, where poor people lived. He said he thought New Haven was more interesting than Yale; he had joined a mixed-race committee that was refurbishing abandoned houses.

When Tom gradually stopped calling her, Marsha had suffered badly. Finally she called him and they went for a last walk. He told her he was seeing someone else. "We met on the Cambridge common. She was walking her dog," he said.

"You're a coward," she said. "You could have told me."

"You're right." He bowed his head in apology, but she thought that if he *had* told her she might have made a scene and embarrassed them both.

Two weeks later, she took nothing to read on a train trip to New York to visit her family. (She had brought the books she'd need for the next chapter of her dissertation, but she deliberately left them in her suitcase.) She gathered her thoughts and tried to follow a slim trail of self-knowledge as it circled more and more deeply into her mind. Riding along the Connecticut shore, looking out at Long Island Sound—flat and gray—she imagined Alan waiting for her at the bottom of a flight of stairs. She felt honest and tired. When the train reached New Haven, she suddenly dragged

her bag off the overhead rack, climbed off the train, and
called him. "Tom and I broke up," she began. They were
still talking half an hour later.

That had been six months ago. Now, in her apartment
in Cambridge, Alan looked down at Marsha, who was still
in bed. Then something distracted him. "I don't know how
you can live in this place without painting it," Alan said,
circling her room. The paint was peeling. It didn't seem
to occur to Alan that he was naked. Marsha always loved
being naked before him, but then she didn't talk about
walls. "I didn't even think of painting," she admitted.

"I like these old-fashioned moldings." He headed for
the shower. He was taking the train back to New Haven
that morning, but she couldn't see him off. As a teaching
fellow, she was leading small groups of undergraduates
through some seventeenth-century poems, and she had to
conduct a tutorial on George Herbert that day. She and
Alan ate breakfast, he dressed and she in her robe, and
suddenly he had to hurry. He gathered his things together—he had a hard Samsonite suitcase she disliked—
kissed her, and left. They couldn't see each other the next
weekend, but on the Thursday after that she was to go to
New Haven for the weekend.

When Marsha made her bed she found Alan's slippers
under it—old blue corduroy with walked-on backs—and
when she brushed her teeth she couldn't find the toothpaste
and realized that in his haste Alan had taken it. She hurried
off to the tutorial, which was in a small room in an old
house near Harvard Yard. It was with five sophomore girls,
who speculated that day instead of simply reading. "Will
you please just *look* at the *lines*?" Marsha said sharply.

"Let him be rich and wearie," said God in the Herbert

poem, speaking of man, to whom He had given all possible blessings except rest. "Restlessness," God pointed out, "may tosse him to my breast." The girls, all friendly, and usually quick, stared at Marsha.

Then Sarah laughed, catching the meaning. "Are we a blessing of yours?" she asked.

"Yes," said Marsha, relaxing. "You're definitely one of my blessings."

"Are *you* restless, even with all your blessings?" Sarah said, smiling at her. "I think today you are a bit restless."

Marsha *was* in a hurry, as if time mattered. "Next week 'Jordan (I),' " she called as they all tramped down the stairs—and then, shouting a line from the poem as she crossed the street, " 'Is there in truth no beautie?' "

She went through the Yard and, beyond it, to the post office on Mount Auburn Street, where she bought a postcard. Leaning on a desk, she addressed the card to Alan. On the other side, in pencil, she wrote in crude, funny letters, "YOU WILL NEVER SEE YOUR SLIPPERS AGAIN UNLESS YOU SURRENDER MY TOOTHPASTE. THE BLACK HAND." She considered drawing a black hand, but it would look like a child's dirty print, so she drew footprints that wound up from the bottom of the card past the letters. It took a while to shade them all with the pencil, but the effect was satisfyingly sinister, and she mailed the card. On the steps of the post office she met Tom.

"Hi," he said. Tom's eyes always reminded her of Bing cherries. The dark parts, which seemed larger and softer than in other people's eyes, were so dark that light flashed off them.

"I'm mailing a present to my aunt," he said. "I bought

her an art book. Would you like to come with me while I mail it?" Marsha laughed and went back inside the post office with Tom—where, anyway, it was warm. It was one of the first cold days of late fall.

"How are you?" she said.

"I miss you."

"How's the dog walker?" She had tried to keep herself from picturing him walking at night with a woman. She imagined someone tall and blond who wore her coat open and led an expensive, unfriendly dog.

"That's up in the air." He reached the head of the line and mailed his package. "Lunch?" he said then. They left the post office and she walked beside him. He was taller and heavier than Alan. She and Tom didn't touch, but she stepped into the chunk of air that was next to him and carved out by his shape, recognizing it in the same way she recognized her winter coat when she put it on for the first time each fall, remembering its weight on her shoulders and how the wool smelled. They went to the Chinese restaurant where they had always gone, and ordered egg foo yung. Tom didn't talk much. Marsha talked about her teaching and her dissertation. After a pause he said, "I'm living with a caracole." He had thick, straight black hair, and now he pushed it back off his forehead, as if to see more clearly how she'd react.

Of course she thought it was a woman. "A *pretty* caracole?" She did know he was teasing.

"Not very."

"All right, what's a caracole?"

"Come back with me and see." He said he was staying in a duplex apartment in Boston, looking after the place while the owner, his thesis adviser, was in Europe. There was a cat he fed, he explained, and for some reason Marsha wondered whether he was just going in and out, feeding the cat, and had only *said* he was living there. They took the train to Boston. She had another tutorial at four. Ordinarily she'd spend the afternoon in her stall at the library.

The cat met them at the door and Tom fed it. The caracole turned out to be a spiral staircase, although Tom said the word also meant a half turn performed by a horse and rider, and before that a snail. He drew a spiral in the air with his finger, and they climbed the narrow metal staircase, which connected the bedroom with the rest of the apartment. The bed was a low, large mattress that took up most of the space in the room, and when they got up there they kissed and held each other for a long time, and then they made love.

"How did you know that word?" said Marsha later.

"I like to read the dictionary," Tom said.

She knew this was true. They were still lying on the mattress, she closer to the top of the staircase, which was an unrailed hole in the floor. They were quiet for a long time. Then Tom said, "I'm thinking about my aunt, the one I sent the present to. Do you want to hear what happened to her?"

"Is it funny?"

"No." He was propped on one elbow, facing her. His eyes were grave.

She kept expecting the professor who owned the apartment to turn up, not in Europe at all, and find them, but she didn't get up. "Tell me."

"Aunt Lucy was a young girl then," he said. "She was

traveling with her mama and papa through the great cities of Europe, and in one city—maybe Vienna or Milan—they bought her a ticket and sent her to the opera alone. Her seat was up in a narrow balcony near the ceiling, in a single row of seats way over on the side. Aunt Lucy could hardly see anything except the opposite front corner of the stage." He told the story as if he knew it by heart.

"At one point—maybe this was a children's show—a clown came out onstage just below her, wearing a sign on his chest. Of course Aunt Lucy couldn't see what the sign said—she could see only a little of *him*. Now, she was sitting almost as far to the right as possible. She had the worst seat in the house. Next to her on her left were two women, and Lucy thought maybe they could see better. After the clown left the stage, she turned and asked the nearer one what the sign said. But the *other* one courteously leaned forward in her seat and twisted around to hear Lucy—and fell over the railing. She fell to the floor of the opera house."

Marsha sucked in her breath. "Did she die?"

"Yes. Lucy still feels bad about it. She once told me it haunted her that while the clown was out there her attention had wandered a little. She thought that if she'd been alert she might have been able to read the sign after all."

"Does that make a difference?"

"Lucy thinks so."

On the ride back to Harvard on the Red Line, Marsha tried to remember what the package Tom had mailed looked like. She couldn't remember the name on it, and wondered whether he had held it out of her sight. In retrospect, it seemed the wrong shape for a book. She didn't believe he had an Aunt Lucy.

If Tom called, Marsha planned to say she would not see him. He didn't call. "Wanting T. bad habit," she wrote in her notebook on the train to New Haven ten days later, on her way to spend the weekend with Alan. Then she drew a rectangle around the letters she had written and filled it in with short dense strokes of her ballpoint pen. She opened George Herbert, and because she had loved him so well he spoke to her: "Is all good structure in a winding stair?"

In New Haven, Alan was impatient. It was Thursday night and the paint store was open late. She was hungry but he insisted they had to buy paint, because he wanted to paint the bedroom the next day. Alan lived in a third-floor apartment they would share when the term was over and Marsha could move. The apartment was mostly wall-papered. "Little *designs*," Alan said, shaking out his fingers and arms as if the small, faded sprigs and twigs and flowers were crawling up and down him. They bought two gallons of off-white flat for the walls and a gallon of white enamel for the woodwork, and then ate at a diner, because when it was this late, for some reason, they always wanted eggs.

"That was some postcard," said Alan, halfway through his scrambled eggs.

She'd forgotten the postcard. She put down her fork. "I didn't bring your slippers!"

"Well, you can have your toothpaste back anyway," he said. "I *guess*." He laughed. "I didn't know *what* I'd done with my slippers. I kept looking for them. And I noticed that I had two tubes of toothpaste, but I thought I forgot and bought it twice."

"We use the same brand."

"Well, the card was funny," he said. "And it kept me pure."

"What do you mean?" Her face grew warm.

He was eating quickly, but he looked pleased with himself. "There's this girl—woman—Donna, who's active on the committee. You'll meet her—there's a party Saturday. And she likes me. The other night, after the meeting, she asked me if she could come over, so we came home, but when I opened the downstairs door, there was the mail lying on the floor, with your postcard right on top, staring up at us, and scary feet all over it."

"Did she read it?"

"Yes. I picked it up and we both read it. She thought it was a riot. But it made things quite clear."

"She didn't know about me?"

"No, I guess not." He put down his fork. "But then she gave me a lecture on how you should move down here as soon as possible. She thinks long-distance relationships are terribly hard."

"She does?" She was angry with this Donna.

"She says it's too hard not to cheat."

Marsha and Alan had never discussed "cheating," but now it came to her that she probably would have used that word, too. He was eating a slice of toast, chewing slowly. "Is it hard for you?" he said. "Actually, it isn't hard for me."

"But you just said my postcard kept you pure."

"Not really," he said. "It was a relief to see it. I'd been

wondering how to keep things from happening without hurting her feelings." The lights in the diner were bright, and the conversation felt public, though no one else was listening.

"If I slept with someone else," he said, "I'd be thinking the whole time of how to tell you. You're the person I tell things to." The Formica table was red. There was spilled sugar on it—Alan took sugar in his coffee—and Marsha ran her finger in it, making a line of red, then a circle. She drank some coffee. She waited to hear what she was going to say but she didn't say anything.

In the morning they painted. Marsha had left old clothes there, and she put them on first thing. Alan was anxious to get started because he had to leave soon—he had classes in the afternoon. They carried their coffee into the bedroom. Alan started taking apart the bookcase—bricks and boards—and Marsha gathered up the bedding and put it out of the way in the living room. They had two paint rollers. They began rolling paint over the wall opposite the bed, but almost immediately the paint-dampened wallpaper—which had seemed so old and fixed that it was part of the wall itself—began to pucker and then to stand away from the wall in large patches.

"I should have known," said Alan. "We'll have to take it off."

Marsha eased her hand under the place where the paper was coming away from the wall and pulled. She was able to remove a scrap about eight inches long. It was satisfying to do this. The wallpaper that came off was thick—there were several layers. Underneath was a yellowish bare wall, stained with ancient glue.

The next piece was not so easy. After a while she brought a spatula from the kitchen. Alan was using a paint scraper that had a razor blade in it. They took the wallpaper off inch by inch. They did not talk much. This work was absorbing. Then, as she dug the spatula under an exposed edge, Marsha said, "Could a person who's sitting down fall over the railing of a balcony? At the theater?"

"I don't think so. Why?"

"Someone told me a story. A woman up high in a theater turns to answer a question. She shifts around with her rear end half off the seat—she needs to talk to someone two seats over." Marsha acted it out, spatula in hand, perched on an imaginary chair. "And she topples over the railing and dies."

"No. There are engineering specifications. The railing would be too high. Was that in a book, or what?"

"No, someone told me. It was in Europe."

"Europeans have common sense, too. Who told you about it?"

"I can't remember," she said.

She did not let herself pull the next piece of wallpaper off until she had loosened a good distance of edge, but still only a small square came when she did pull. "This will take forever," she said.

"Yes." And Alan had to go to class. For the afternoon, Marsha was alone, peeling wallpaper. Sometimes she wandered—to the bathroom, to the kitchen for coffee or a cookie. She turned over papers on Alan's desk and found her postcard. There were no secrets. The other papers were the syllabus of one of his courses and the schedule of a film series. Back in the bedroom she worked hard, so Alan would be impressed. As she worked, in her mind she told Alan the details about the woman who fell from the theater seat.

"Do you think it would make a difference if Aunt Lucy's attention wandered?" she asked.

"Where did he *get* this story?" she imagined Alan saying. Together, they figured out Tom. "I don't know why I keep thinking about him," said Marsha. But then, in fact, she began to think of him some more—Tom calling her the following week when she was back in Cambridge, and Tom in the future, dropping in to see them in a house in some distant city. She had a child—Alan's child. Tom admired her child.

When Alan returned, he had been given good advice. "There are machines to do this," he said, and went to the phone. They rented a wallpaper steamer—a huge, dark metal contraption, which they lugged up to the third floor. The steamer had a tank that held water and heated it. When the water boiled, Alan pressed a metal plate against the wall and squeezed a handle to release steam. Marsha followed him with the scraper. It was smelly and dirty, but the task was easy now. They stripped two walls. Alan went out for hamburgers and brought them back. Marsha took a shower. After they ate she was too tired to do more, and the bedroom was too messy to sleep in, so they dragged the mattress into the living room and Alan put the sheet back on it and wordlessly eased Marsha down. He undressed her and rubbed her back and shoulders. Then they made love and fell asleep.

•

Marsha had been eager to go to the housing committee's party, a potluck lunch, but on the way, the next day, she was seized with a prodigious shyness. They had finished removing the wallpaper. After the party was over, they would come back for the machine and return it to the rental store. The lunch was in the apartment of one of the black women on the committee. "I'll say the wrong thing," Marsha said. "She'll think I'm a bigot."

"That's all right. Clara thinks everybody's a bigot," Alan said.

They stopped to buy apple cider, his contribution. Waiting while he paid, Marsha studied her reflection in the door of the cooler. Her skin felt dry and permanently stained and shrunken from old wallpaper glue. She stared at the shadowy woman pierced by rows of soda bottles. Tom had never taken her to parties.

But it was all right. Coats were piled on a bed she could glimpse off a corridor. Plates of food were lined up on a table. This was not like one of the confusing parties people her own age sometimes gave, at which she was always afraid she might do the wrong thing; this was like visiting one of her aunts. Marsha was introduced around and filled her plate with fried chicken and sat next to Alan on a sofa. A young black man drifted over to them. "He's deep," he said to Marsha.

"I'm sorry?"

"Deep," he said. He gestured toward Alan, who was being talked to by an earnest white woman in her forties. "He never said he had a girl. We were worried about him. We thought we'd have to fix him up."

"*I* don't think Alan's deep," Marsha said. The man had

pulled over a hassock so he could sit and talk to her. She saw that he was curious about her. "I can figure him out every time."

The man laughed. "No, no, Alan's the mystery man. That's why my mom made sure he was coming—so she could keep an eye on him."

He told her his name was Terry. This was his mother's apartment, he said, pointing at Clara, a thin, sharp-faced woman in her fifties whom Marsha had just met.

"It's a nice apartment," she said, "but I just can't keep from thinking about the wallpaper." The living room had beige wallpaper with a dark-red intricate design on it.

"You don't like the wallpaper?"

"It's not that." She told him how she and Alan had spent the last day and a half. "I can't help it," she finished. "I keep looking for places where you could start a good rip. Right behind you—where the seam is. See? There's a little pucker. Sometimes you can get in under one. . . ."

Suddenly she was perfectly happy. It was not just because Terry was friendly, but she didn't know what else it was. Just then a young woman came hurrying in, arms laden—a big white woman, tall and heavy, with blond hair down to her hips and wearing a navy-blue cloak. "Clara, I brought layer cake," she called, and Clara turned around.

"Well, I was just giving up on you, Donna," she said.

"That's Donna?" said Marsha. "That's not how I pictured her." Marsha never talked loudly, but this time she did, and everyone looked at her.

"How did you picture me?" Donna said. "Did Alan tell you I made a play for him?"

This was so close to what Alan had said that Marsha could not answer, but it didn't matter, because somehow

Donna had turned the group—twelve or fifteen people, until now in clusters and pairs—into a single audience, as some gifted partygoers can.

"I have to tell you about this lady," she said, unbuttoning her cloak. "I have to tell you about this *postcard*. I went over to Alan's—I think Alan's irresistible." There was laughter. "And there's his mail in the hall, and this post-card that says—what did it say? 'If you don't give back my toothpaste you'll never see your slippers again.' Like a ransom note? It was signed, 'The Black Hand.' "

"Black hand?" said Terry. "Like black people?"

"I think I meant pirates," said Marsha. Nothing like this had ever happened to her before.

"Pirates," said Terry thoughtfully. "Pirates."

But after a few more minutes, as they were finishing their cake, Alan looked at his watch. They just had time to return the wallpaper steamer to the rental store. Marsha talked all the way back to the apartment. She talked about Terry and Clara. "I don't think she thought I was a bigot," she said.

"She probably did," Alan said, "but it's OK." He parked his car and they hurried up to the apartment, and Alan lifted the huge wallpaper steamer. "I'll go first," said Marsha, running down to the second-floor landing. She couldn't calm herself.

At the landing she looked up. The staircase had a turn in it, and for a moment she could hear the bumping of the machine but couldn't see Alan, and then he came slowly around the corner.

"You know, Alan," she said steadily, looking at him, speaking more slowly now, "I slept with Tom again last week." But as she spoke his foot slipped on a loose tread and he tripped. He didn't fall but did a quick shuffle and stumbled down, straight toward her, trying to control the descent of the heavy machine, and Marsha didn't get out of the way but foolishly raised her arms to catch him—which she did, in fact, though the wallpaper steamer bruised her ankle—while what she had said, no longer private and potent, seemed to pause in the air between them, the way their delighted child would, one day: tossed high but catchable.

THE

CROSSWORD

PUZZLE

Once someone asked me whether Anita was my mother, and another time someone thought she was my older sister, but we're just friends. We met when we started working in the same office— a large law firm—on the same day, typing names and addresses into a computer. After we'd typed for a while without talking, except for hello, Anita said, "Beat you to a James." She had fluffy red hair and lots of rings.

"A James?" I thought it was slang I didn't know.

"*James.* Long for Jim. Bet you I get to one first." We were typing from stacks of cards, copying the information at the top and then turning them over.

"Oh," I said. She did, too: she found a James after three more cards.

"Now Mary," I said in a challenging voice, but

she won again. We went to lunch together. At lunch she did the *New York Times* crossword puzzle before she'd talk, but it took her only a few minutes.

In fact I'd seen Anita before the day in the office, but I didn't recognize her. About a year ago, I was running on her street with my dog. We passed a big old house, and a woman was carrying in her groceries. A dog ran out, a skinny Irish setter, one of those dogs that moves so smoothly in curves you think its spine is made of rubber. He came running after my dog, Misty, and the woman chased after us in her heels, shouting, "Oliver! Oliver!"

"He's emotionally disturbed," she said, panting, when she caught up to me. "I'll never get him home. He sneaked past me when he saw your dog." She looked annoyed with me. "Would you mind coming back?" Oliver was sniffing Misty's backside, and sure enough, he followed us, but the woman still couldn't catch him. When she reached for him he shrank away and jumped sideways. In the end Misty and I had to go into her house and walk all the way down a long hall before Oliver slipped in after us and the woman closed the door. It was a dark house. I had a sense of old, good things and many rooms, and it felt wrong to be there in my sweaty running clothes. I was a little frightened, inside a house—deep inside—with a stranger.

"The breeder *begged* me to adopt him," the woman said. I nodded and moved forward but it was a while before I could leave. She kept talking. You'd think I'd have recognized her when I saw her again, but I didn't.

The day we met, when Anita finished the crossword puzzle at lunch, she said, "You interest me." I was surprised because I'd been trying all morning to do everything right, starting a new job, and I felt childish. I attempted to describe myself with a little pizzazz, but all I could think to tell her was that Kevin, my husband, and I were trying to have a baby. Her eyes softened when I said it, which was interesting to *me*, because I'd been seeing her as someone whose eyes were always hard, who'd say things like "Her number was up" if somebody died. Telling her about the baby that didn't come wasn't exactly like talking about a death, but almost. I'd been feeling as if I were the mother of a long line not of dead babies but of little monthly dead eggs, little dabs of stuff I imagined as tiny subpets, what people might keep when they didn't even want a gerbil, much less a dog.

"Have you been doing word processing for a long time?" I asked Anita. I thought she probably had typed all her life. I've taken a lot of college courses at night, but I'm a dynamite typist—I worry that I'll never do anything as well.

"If I'm going to process words," Anita said, "I always think I should wear a green smock and a hairnet, and bad-smelling juice should spurt out of the words when I process them." I laughed.

"No, this isn't me," she went on. "I managed an office for fifteen years, and I once had a radio program. But there's less stress this way. I'm fifty-five—I don't need a job to give me a sense of power. Women in their fifties run the world."

"Do you like being fifty-five?" I asked her. I'd wondered about older women.

"Well, look at *you*, sister," she said. "I bet you're running to the bathroom every ten minutes to check. Once a month your life gets ruined by a stain in your panties. Who's in better shape, huh?"

When I remember what she said, I'm surprised that I wasn't hurt or embarrassed, but it came out softly and—in a way—sweetly. I kept waiting for her to say more in that tone, in fact. It was as if she'd lowered her head and were talking *under* something.

When I'd known Anita for a month or two, there was a Saturday when Kevin was away. My period had been five days late, and I'd been thinking hard about a baby. I always get carried away. That morning I discovered I wasn't pregnant, though, and I called Anita. I don't know why I called her instead of one of my girlfriends. It's a mystery, I suppose, who we lean on.

Anita said she was cleaning out closets and I should come over. I was to take a shower and put on old clothes and leave the breakfast dishes and that's what I did. I spent hours that day lying on her bed, listening to her talk while she sorted out her dresses and hats and shoes. I began to feel better.

When I'd arrived, Anita took me in her arms at the door and held me against her shoulder like a mother in a book, and I looked past her—at Oliver and the house—and realized that she was the woman with the dog. I didn't say so, though. I'd often thought about that woman, but I'd remembered her as a little older and fatter than Anita, and a little crazier. Now I tried to merge them into one in my mind, but for some time after that, when I thought of the woman with the dog, I'd have to rearrange her in my head to turn her into Anita.

.

Now it is early on a Sunday evening in May. The sidewalk where I am walking is covered with tender, light green polly-noses—maple wings, someone told me they're actually called. I am carrying a plate covered with aluminum foil. I pass a little girl and her mother sitting on their front steps.

"Where is that lady going?" asks the girl. "What is on her plate? Why is she carrying a plate?"

"*I* don't know," says the mother. "How should *I* know?"

There are dinner rolls on the plate, and I'm carrying them to Anita's house. She's invited me to dinner. I recently learned to make these rolls, which are made with yeast. You have to knead the dough and let them rise twice. They're very good, now that I'm doing it right. At first I was too impatient, and I didn't understand that they wouldn't rise in the oven like biscuits.

I haven't looked forward to dinner at Anita's tonight, but I couldn't think of a reason to say no. Now I'm pleased, though. I like being by myself for a few minutes, between Kevin and Anita. Nobody knows where I am, I say to myself, though both of them could make a pretty accurate guess. If I turned right instead of walking straight ahead, I could walk away from everyone forever. But I have nothing with me except the plate, not even my pocketbook. In my new life I'd have to live on dinner rolls. I picture myself, in my red pants, walking east into a neighborhood I don't know, taking a roll whenever I'm hungry.

When Anita comes to the door I see that she's dressed up, wearing a print dress in many colors, predominantly lilac. She seizes the plate and hurries into the kitchen. "Still warm!" she calls. Oliver snarls at me, though I have been here several times.

Now that I'm in Anita's house again, I'm glad of it. There is a breezy room at the back with plants and louvered windows. I sink down on a couch there and take off my shoes. Oliver lies down in a corner, his paws stuck out in front of him as if he's numbering his grievances on his toes. Anita offers me a beer but I ask for a Coke. She brings it and goes away again. On the table in front of me is the Sunday *Times* crossword puzzle.

"You didn't finish the puzzle!" I call out.

Anita runs in from the kitchen. "That's because I was cooking for you. I didn't let myself start until I had everything under control."

She must have been doing the puzzle when I arrived. I came too early. "Do you want me to be quiet for a while so you can finish it?" I say.

She comes forward, puts down a pot holder, and settles into a chair opposite me with the puzzle and her red pen. She always says red shows up better against the black. I know that she has no choice but to finish the puzzle and that I mustn't help her. Once, I looked over her shoulder and saw something I knew.

" 'Chastity's mother' is 'Cher,' " I said.

Anita raised her hand as if to slap me. " 'Chastity's mother' is 'Cher' in about three puzzles a week. It's a trick that's worn thin—you're supposed to think it's a Greek goddess."

"I didn't know," I said.

"And helping someone do the puzzle is like helping someone finish a box of chocolates."

So now I drink my Coke and keep quiet. I wonder what the pot holder was about to grasp and whether whatever it was is burning. I wouldn't mind reading another section of the paper, but I don't see any more of it.

Anita fills in the answers to the crossword puzzle as quickly as if she were writing her name over and over. "This one isn't bad," she says presently. "It's not as disgustingly easy as some."

At one point she says, " 'Lighthouse' backwards," and at another, "Roman numerals . . ." But she can't finish it. There's a corner that contains one phrase she can't figure out, even though she has many of the letters. "I have to get the long one," she says. "I don't know these rivers."

"You wouldn't look them up."

"No."

She finally tells me the clue, "sub rosa." I think I know what that means but I can't express it.

" 'Hidden'?" I say timidly.

"Forget it," she says. She sits there for a while longer and I see that she is angry—with me or the puzzle or herself. I go into the kitchen to see if I can figure out what's cooking, and she breaks away and follows me. "What are you doing? Are you hungry? I don't think the chicken is done yet."

I am hungry. "Do you want me to make a salad?"

"No." Anita offers me another Coke but I say no and stay in the kitchen, sitting on a stool, and she finds her own beer, left there a while ago, and takes out the salad bowl herself.

"It couldn't be 'hidden,' " she says. "It's something with a twist to it. A joke. That's the trouble with you, Laurie. You take everything literally." She shakes her head, but she sounds affectionate. "Even so, I like doing for you. Carry this into the dining room, will you?"

Anita is not my only friend in the office. The other one is Jasper Korn, a lawyer who started there about when we did. He's in his late thirties but this is his first job as a lawyer. He worked for his father, who has an upholstery business, and went to law school at night. Jasper and I met at the copy machine his first day and discovered we'd both gotten into trouble for the same mistake—mixing up two people in the office named Pat, a woman lawyer and a man paralegal. The woman Pat had yelled at me and almost yelled at Jasper. "Yell isn't exactly the right word," he said. "But she *looked askance*. She *took a dim view*." That seemed like something Anita would say but she didn't like him.

"His shirt billows up and he doesn't stuff it back down into his pants," she said. "It's because he twists when he moves. He looks this way and that way."

Once when Jasper was finishing a brief in a hurry he asked me if I could stay late and type. I was delighted. I couldn't be quite casual about him—I always could say exactly when we'd last talked, and I remembered what we'd said. It wasn't sexual. I often felt like touching him, but only to straighten him up. I'm not looking for someone. But there's that good middle category: men you don't stay up nights thinking about but who seem more definitely placed before your eyes than most men, as if they're in bold type.

After a few weeks I was promoted to typing for the lawyers. I told Anita she'd surely be moved, too, but she wasn't. I sit in a different cubicle now, and once a month or so I end up staying late, working on something with Jasper.

We work well together. We kid around about how hard he finds writing, or about the case. He teases me. We have one of those dumb office jokes that mean you're friends— I'm taller than he is and somebody once called out, "Hey, look—it's *Annie Hall*," so we started to say, "Hey, Woody?" and "Yes, Diane?"

Once Jasper and I were on our way over to McDonald's, where we sometimes have a quick supper on our long evenings, and I happened to mention Anita.

"Oh, God," he said, and then, "Oh, no—now I have to tell you what I meant, don't I? I'm such an idiot."

"What are you talking about?"

"They're watching Anita."

"Who's watching her?"

"Larry and Steve," said Jasper. They're two of the partners in the firm. "You know, Laurie, they're not all that pleased with Anita to start with."

"She's very good," I said.

"Apparently she always gets one thing wrong," said Jasper, "but it's basic—so the work has to be done over."

I knew this had happened once or twice, but *always* seemed like an exaggeration.

"Is that why they're watching her?" I said. We were on line in McDonald's by this time.

"Well, no, I'm the guilty party here," Jasper said, lowering his voice. "I told them about something I saw. One day I came into the office—I'd come back early from lunch. There were a few people around—you were in the library, I think—but Anita was the only person I saw, and she wasn't near her desk. She was going through . . . well, through other women's pocketbooks."

I had to order just then. I asked for a hamburger as if nothing had happened, but my hands felt prickly.

"Whose pocketbooks?"

"One was Edie's—and the other was yours. *That* one."

I tightened my hand on the shoulder strap. It was a red leather bag I'd bought a few months ago. It would have been hanging on the back of my chair. Edie sits near me. She's about Anita's age, quiet and hard to get to know.

My order had come and I opened the bag to pay for it, relieved, for a second, when my hand went right to my wallet. Then I realized that of course I'd used the bag many times since the day Jasper was talking about. I felt angry with him. I hated feeling angry with Jasper. When we sat down, I said, "She's welcome to look in my bag. Maybe she needed a tissue. We're *friends*." He didn't answer. "Did she know you saw her?" I said.

"I think so." He looked troubled—he suddenly looked like his father, whom I'd met once: his face looked smaller than usual and had lines in it. "She moved very smoothly from your bag to the file cabinet, but it was a little *too* smooth."

·

Now, in Anita's house, the chicken is finally cooked. I set the table, as if I were her daughter, while Anita makes a salad. She talks about the office—how much she doesn't like Jasper, actually. "There's something sneaky about him," she says. We sit down to our meal and she raises her glass—she has opened a bottle of wine. "I'm pretty sure you're pregnant," she says casually.

"How do you know?" I am instantly certain—superstitiously—that she is right. But I am stunned.

"Skin tones," says Anita. "I'm the oldest of eight kids—I had plenty of practice."

I haven't been letting myself calculate dates but even so I know perfectly well that my period is one day late. I haven't even spoken this news aloud to Kevin. I haven't exactly *thought* it. I begin to eat my chicken with an odd lightness, as if the knife and fork—which are actually quite solid—have become weightless. But for some reason I don't want to talk about being pregnant.

Anita has a large dining room table and we are isolated at one end of it. She has lit two candles and centered them, though. I look around at the other chairs. All I know of her family life is that she was once married briefly, had no children, and that the house used to belong to her in-laws. "You never talk about brothers and sisters," I say. "Do they live around here?"

"The wrong ones live around here."

"You don't get along with them?"

"I'm hard to get along with," Anita says. "Your friend Jasper thinks I'm impossible to get along with."

I need to change the subject again. "You get along with *other* people at work," I say. "You get along with Edie." Only after I have spoken do I see where my mind has taken me and yet I cannot stop, like someone who must touch a wound. "In some ways you seem close to her."

This isn't even true. Edie is faceless—no one could seem close to her. I don't know what I'm after. Do I want Anita to say that she and Edie are such good friends that Edie lets her look into her purse?

"I can't be friends with someone who has so little style,"

Anita says. "I don't even *mean* style. She doesn't pick out her clothes—did you know that? Edie's sister is retired, and every morning she goes to Macy's bargain basement. She shops for Edie, too."

"Every morning?"

"I couldn't stand not picking out my own clothes," says Anita. "Her purse was her mother's. Edie's mother died a week after buying a new purse. That brown purse with the metal clasp?"

I am confused, and Anita is looking at me, almost as if she can read what I'm thinking. "Well, if her mother died . . ." I say weakly, but Anita jumps up.

"I forgot the rolls!" she says. "Your wonderful rolls." She runs into the kitchen, and then I hear her call out with real alarm, and I follow her. Oliver has stolen the rest of the chicken from its platter on the counter and is finishing off a breast, crunching the bones and growling at Anita.

"I'll take it away from him," I say. I've sometimes had to reach into Misty's throat to take away a sharp bone and she always lets me.

But Anita is crouched down, trying to open Oliver's jaw. "Damn it," she is saying in a low voice. "Damn it, damn it." And then Oliver bites her, and she topples over backward and sits on the floor in her pretty dress like a child. "It'll puncture his stomach," she says. "The bone will kill him." She is holding one hand, where the bite is, with the other, crying a little.

Oliver has fled, so I pick up what's left of the chicken and put it out of his reach. I follow him. He is in a corner near the stairs but when I approach he growls. Then he runs upstairs. I go back to Anita and help her up. "He'll be fine," I say. "It's only a possibility that bones hurt them.

It doesn't *usually* happen." I don't actually know anything about it. "After all," I say, thinking fast, "dogs who go outside a lot get into garbage, and it doesn't seem to harm them." I take her hand to examine the bite.

Anita looks up at me. She is not crying now, but her eyes look soft, with the softness I remember from that first conversation about the baby. "I was looking for money," she says.

"I know," I answer, helping her up, putting my arm around her. I haven't yet noticed what I mean.

GO,

MERCY

"If you have two people," said Matt, talking fast
and counting the two people on his fingers, "there
are three possible groupings. Do you see, Dad?
One person alone, the other person alone, or the
two of them together. Right?"

"I suppose so," said Linda, his mother, because she thought her husband might not answer.
It was almost dinnertime, and Linda was making
eggplant lasagna. She'd steamed the slices of
eggplant and now she was layering everything in
a large, flat pan: noodles, eggplant, cheese, tomato sauce. Zo, the oldest child, who was coming
home from college any minute for the start of his
winter break (it was a week before Christmas),
liked lasagna, but the eggplant was to please
Gina, their daughter, the vegetarian.

"Now with *three* people," said Matt, "it's a lot

more complicated. That's how it came up—the Family Life Unit. Why we shouldn't make babies." He giggled. Young for his age, he was embarrassed by the high school's cautionary lessons about smoking, drinking, drugs, and sex, but Linda thought he was also flattered. "If there are three people," he was saying, "there are seven possible combinations. All three people, persons one and two, persons one and three . . ."

"All right," said his father. "So what?"

"It's why family life is complicated," said Matt.

"Oh, all right," said Dennis, his father, with a loud, wrong emphasis to his voice, which Matt seemed to ignore, a tone Linda had heard occasionally all through this hard fall, during which a strange sadness had fallen upon Dennis—unless the sadness had started earlier; it was hard to remember. That odd tone sometimes made her think of something that it wasn't connected to: as a young nursing student, Linda had proctored final exams for pocket money, and near the end of each exam, after almost three hours of tense quiet, during which the students wrote ceaselessly, she had to say, "You have seven minutes left. You have seven minutes left." She remembered how it felt to speak out into the deep silence, and how the students, hearing her, would jump.

"But what I want to know is," Matt was saying, "what's the formula?"

"What formula?" Dennis had been leaning on the kitchen counter, drumming the fingers of one hand on its surface, but now he sat down at the table.

"Dad, there's *got* to be a formula. How do you figure the possible combinations for four people, or five—look, there are five of us, and there could be you and Mom alone, you and Mom and Zo, you and Mom and Gina, Mom and Gina and Zo . . ."

"Is that an assignment?" said his father, with his own voice, but sounding a little confused.

"No, I'm just curious," said Matt. "Four people is fifteen combinations. I counted. It goes up fast."

Gina came into the room. She looked at Matt but didn't ask what he was talking about. Gina looked confident. She was tall and had long dark hair cut straight across the middle of her back, and square glasses. She had graduated from high school in June, second in her class, and had won a scholarship to Barnard, but she'd come home three weeks after the start of her freshman year, weepy. At first, Linda had blamed the college, then wondered whether Gina was unhappily in love or even pregnant, but her daughter shook such suggestions off. "That would be stupid, and I'm not stupid," she said impatiently. She'd stayed at home, mostly, since then, except for a baby-sitting job and an art course she took twice a week. Now she said she was going back to school in January.

"And with Dennis in such bad shape right now, too," Linda had said to a friend in the hospital cafeteria one day, telling her about Gina, but then had the thought— or maybe her friend had said it, or merely *thought* it— that Gina would be fine if only Dennis were fine.

They'd had a warm October, and every day, after Dennis left for his office—he was a doctor—and Matthew went to school, Gina had taken a kitchen chair and a book or a sketch pad out to their short city front yard when the sun crossed it in the morning, and then moved the chair as the sun moved, until the sun was snapped up by a tall square building across the street. By the time the sun got caught, Gina would be sitting on the sidewalk, where friends of hers sometimes passed, girls she'd known in high school who were at Southern Connecticut now. When their side of the street was in shade, she'd pick up the chair and carry it back inside, its slatted back tucked under her right arm, her book in her left, her long hair reaching almost to the chair back, a hurried look on her face. Linda, a private duty nurse, had been home herself in October, between jobs, but then she'd started working again. Now Zo would be around for a few weeks. He was driving home—he'd recently bought a used car—and he'd probably walk in the door talking: he'd liven things up. Zo was in his third year at the University of Vermont; he had friends, adventures, stories to tell.

Gina was not technically a vegetarian, as she often explained, but an ovo-lacto-vegetarian. Ordinarily, if the rest of them had meat, she'd fix herself something with tofu, or a grilled cheese sandwich, but Linda had wanted her to feel more included than that tonight, so she'd found the recipe for the eggplant lasagna. Just as it was ready to go into the oven, Zo arrived, smiling and—sure enough— talking. He was excited about his car, which they'd never seen, and he made all of them come out in the cold to look at it. It was an old Plymouth Duster. "Terrific old cars," he kept saying to Dennis. He wanted to take them for a ride around the block, and Matt agreed.

"I made good time from Burlington," Zo said, coming

in with Matt for the second time. "It's a great car. I just can't *believe* I have a car." He laughed at himself a little.

Turning, Linda saw Dennis looking at Zo hungrily, his face thrust forward as if he were taking in information, as if an important number were going to appear on Zo's forehead. "I can't remember when I last *enjoyed* something," Dennis had said to her in bed the night before, and she'd spent much of the day trying to pin down the last date on which Dennis had definitely had a good time. She remembered a minor-league baseball game in Burlington when they'd driven Zo up for his freshman year, how the home-team pitcher had a no-hitter that lasted until the second out of the ninth inning, and how they all stood to applaud the man when he came up to bat in the eighth, Dennis's big hands clapping slowly together, a sly smile breaking his face, as if the no-hitter were indeed a secret, for he'd cautioned Matt not to mention it—not saying anything himself but pointing elaborately at the scoreboard until the boy caught on.

"But you don't have to panic," he'd said last night. "I gave my word to Bill Slater, too." Bill Slater was a psychiatrist, an old medical school classmate whom Dennis had finally phoned.

The ball game had been almost two and a half years ago. She remembered other occasions—a walk in the park, a meal in a restaurant, but it was hard to date them. The walk had been in winter, and Dennis sang. The park had been empty except for them.

Now Linda served the lasagna. It was a little unusual, she thought, but good anyway. Zo scraped the cheese off his slices of eggplant, ate the cheese, and left the eggplant at the side of his plate. Immediately Gina speared it with her fork and ate it. "So how's the art?" Zo said to her as they ate.

"It's all right," she said. "Actually, I'm good at it."

"Still Gina," said Zo. "My sister with the swelled head. Let's see."

Gina slapped his shoulder playfully as she put down her fork and went for her sketch pad. Zo pretended to wince, his brown eyes—which were just a little too close together—full of teasing and awkwardness. "My sister the brain," he'd always said—but he *wanted* it that way, Linda thought.

Still, when the sketchbook was brought, he was telling Linda about his part-time job and what he hoped to buy with the money, and more about the car, and he held the pad in his hand without seeming to see it. Then he put it aside, reaching for more lasagna.

"My roommate needed a ride to the airport yesterday and I took him," he was saying. "I almost ran out of gas. The gauge was actually below empty. Before, I'd gotten down to the bottom edge of the little mark, but this time I could see *space* between the little mark and the needle. I was running on grunts. I kept going *uhh, uhh,* as if that was going to make a difference."

"What finally happened?" said Matt.

"I came to a gas station," Zo said. "The Lord sent down a gas station."

Dennis looked at Zo and said quietly, "I've done that before." Zo looked expectantly at his father, as if a story were coming, but Dennis said nothing more, and now Matt was pulling the sketch pad out from under his brother's elbow. He began turning the pages. Linda had looked at Gina's sketches just the other day. She'd been surprised at how good they were.

"Hey, Matt, you've seen it," said Gina. "You'll just get tomato sauce on it."

"No, I won't. I haven't seen this one," he said. It was a sketch of Dennis reading the newspaper, his right hand stroking his ear, a characteristic gesture.

"Let me see that," Dennis said, and he took the sketchbook. He looked at it for a long time, but didn't say anything.

"Well?" said Gina, as he handed the pad back to Zo.

"What do you mean, well?"

"What do you think of it?" she said.

"What do you want," said Dennis abruptly—loudly. "For me to join the crowd and say you're a genius?"

Gina said quickly, "I'm not a genius. I'm smart—I can't help getting good marks. You were the same way, Dad." But she seemed close to tears, and then, her voice breaking as she started to cry, said, "I just thought you might like it."

Linda reached across the table for Gina's arm, but Matt began to talk before she could say anything. He'd remembered his question about combinations of people and had begun to explain it to Zo. "Say if you've got five people, there could be just one of them present, or any two, or any three . . . you know."

"I *don't* know," said Zo. "Is it a game?"

Matt explained again. Gina, who hadn't heard Matt talk about it before, stopped crying and looked interested, and even Dennis was paying attention. Gina said, "Maybe it's one of those factorial things, five times four times three. . . ."

"No," said Matt. "I tried that."

"We could just count," said Zo. "For five people—well, there's all five together, that's one, and there are—let's see, how many combinations of four?"

"Five," said Gina. "Each one of the five people could be missing."

They had finished dinner. Linda hadn't made dessert—it was rare for her to cook something as complicated as the lasagna—but nobody left the table for a while. Then Dennis got up and walked into the living room. No one could figure out the formula Matt wanted to know, and Zo began to talk about something Matt's question had reminded him of, a game he'd played in a drama workshop he'd attended at the university.

"It was something like charades," he said. "We were divided into teams, and one person had to do mime—he had to act out something the other team had thought up. I had to act out having my sick cat put to sleep."

"How did you do it?" said Matt.

"I had a lot of trouble. After a while we got silly," he said, "and people began doing cheers for their team—old high school cheers. You'd be surprised at some of those cheers people remembered from different schools."

"Well, *I* just happen to know the world's *best* high school cheer," Gina said. She had been sitting with the sketch pad in front of her, her hands folded on it as if to keep it from being opened, but now—as if she'd deliberately thrown off her mood—she jumped to her feet and started chanting, thrusting her fist in the air in rhythm:

> *B-E-A-T! Beat 'em! Beat 'em!*
> *B-U-S-T! Bust 'em! Bust 'em!*
> *Beat 'em, bust 'em, that's our custom—*
> *Go . . . o . . . o . . . o, Mercy!*

And she leaped up and flung her arms into the air like a cheerleader.

Linda had stood up to put the leftover lasagna into the refrigerator. "Where did you learn that?" she said, laughing. Gina smoothed her hair and sat down again, panting, flicking the heavy hair behind her chair back.

"That's wild," said Zo.

"Beat 'em, bust 'em, go *mercy*?" said Matt. "It doesn't *sound* very merciful."

"That's why I like it," said Gina. "It was Mercy High School. We once played a soccer game there. I don't know why I remembered the cheer. Sometimes I can't get it out of my head."

"Did you win?" said Zo.

"I don't think so. But it was a great cheer."

"Really."

It was Matt's night to wash the dishes. When Linda had finished putting away the leftovers, she went into the living room, where Dennis had turned on the television and was watching a movie, sitting forward on the sofa as if he hadn't made up his mind whether to keep it on.

"What is that?" said Linda.

"I'm not sure. It's an old film."

She sat down next to him and tried to make sense of the movie. A couple with English accents was arguing—the man was supposed to go somewhere but the woman thought it was unsafe. Maybe it was wartime. Dennis shifted his legs—he wanted to stretch out—so Linda moved to a chair across the room. Behind the crisp voices of the actors on the screen, Linda could hear her children in the kitchen, where the boys were learning Gina's cheer.

"Beat 'em, bust 'em," Gina repeated patiently. "That's our custom." And then they all did it together.

Dennis stood up and turned off the television. "It's good to have Zo home," he said. Then he lay down on the sofa again, reaching for the newspaper, which had been lying on the floor.

"What do you think of his car?" Linda asked.

"Fine, for his purposes."

"He's so pleased." Zo had always accepted himself, as if he were his own affectionate uncle.

But Dennis didn't answer, and then Linda saw that he had fallen asleep, or at least closed his eyes, stretched on the sofa with the newspaper in his hand. She took the paper away from him and began to read it. She hadn't had a chance to see it all day. She took off her shoes and then her feet got cold, so she thought about it for a few minutes, too tired to move, but then talked herself into going upstairs to her bedroom for her slippers. Actually, she was cold all over, and she put on her bathrobe as well, over her pants and sweater, and tied it closed. It was an old plaid bathrobe she'd had since the children were little.

As she came down again, she could hear Zo, still in the kitchen with the others, talking. "No," he was saying, "that won't be any fun. It'll be my first day of vacation. I want to do something *terrific*."

"I have school," Matt said.

"We'll wait for you," said Zo. Linda couldn't imagine

what wonderful plan they could come up with. Zo usually slept, his first day home, then began calling old girlfriends.

"Well, I guess we could always rob a bank," came Gina's cool voice now.

"Oh, *that's* a good idea," said Zo, deadpan. "Which bank?"

"Let's see—last time we robbed the People's Bank on Whitney Avenue," Gina said lightly, "and that was nice. But I've always wanted to rob the Union Trust. Those black and white checkerboard tiles on the floor and the tellers in old-fashioned cages."

They had always understood one another's games and jokes without explanations, even when Linda had taken a while to catch on; and yet this was a little different. Their voices had a certain earnestness—not as if they were really going to rob a bank, of course, but as if—Linda gave it up. She didn't know.

"That's a great idea," Matt was saying. "We'll rob the Union Trust. We'll use Zo's car as a getaway car."

"You don't use your *own car*," said Gina. "You *steal* a car."

"Oh, of course," said Matt. "How do we do that?"

"Well," said Zo, "the best thing might just be to hold somebody up—say a car that's stopped for a traffic light— or maybe not, that's probably too hard." He paused, and Linda, still listening, knew how he'd dip his head and bring it up again, eyes bright, as if to flip an idea up from the back of his mind. "Maybe just a car in a parking lot," he went on eagerly. "We go to some little shopping center out in Hamden—not a big one, just one of those little ones. And we wait until someone goes into a store. And then when he comes out, we steal his car."

"What do we do with *him*?" said Matt.

"We'll have to kill him, I guess," said Gina. Linda had sat down with the newspaper again. She glanced at Dennis, but he was still asleep, turned face down now on the sofa. Linda and her sisters—she had no brothers—had joked constantly, growing up, but they wouldn't have talked quite this way, taken it quite this far.

"Right. How do we kill him?" Zo said cheerfully.

"Shoot him."

"Beat 'em, bust 'em . . ." said Matt, starting *that* up again.

"Yeah, right, we know, we know. But how do we get a gun?" Zo said.

"Oh," said Gina, and she paused for a second or two, in a new way. "A gun is easy to get. I know where there's a gun."

And she spoke with such authority—though her voice seemed suddenly *younger*—that the game was over. There was silence for a moment in the kitchen, and Linda started to push the newspaper aside and jump to her feet, to hurry in there, but then she stopped herself and stayed where she was. After another moment Zo came slowly into the living room. He glanced at his father, who still lay with the back of his head up, his hair—brown but just starting to gray—trimmed neatly at his neck. Zo said he might as well bring in his duffel bag, which he'd left in the trunk of his car. He stopped in the hall for his jacket and Linda heard him step outside, closing the front door behind him carefully so it didn't make much noise. Now Gina came out of the kitchen carrying her sketchbook, her face tipped forward so her hair fell in a thick screen, and she hurried up the stairs. Then

Linda heard Matt, who was alone in the kitchen now, talking to himself about washing the dishes. "All right, Matthew, old buddy," he said out loud. "It's time for deeds of bravery and derring-do," and he clattered the dishes and silverware and began to run the water in the sink.

LIBERTY

APPLES

"You're definitely better off," I said. Julie and I had been arguing for months about George Friedman, the man she'd been seeing. Now he'd broken up with her.

But Julie shook her head. "You don't understand," she said, not for the first time.

I tried, in my imagination, to understand George. "You look pretty, sitting on my floor," I said. She looked irresistible. My husband once said Julie's eyes were too close together, but I love her face. I draw it all the time. We were in my studio, at the top of the house. Our daughters were listening to music downstairs. Out of habit, I'd sat down on my chair—the only one—and Julie's neat, brown-haired head (maybe three gray hairs) was near my hand. "I think I'll keep you as an ornament."

"I'd make a good paperweight," said Julie.

She was drinking her tea eagerly, and now she gathered the wadded, wet tissues around her and stood to throw them into the wastebasket, tugging the short skirt of her dress into place. "I should go." But she picked up my drawing pad and began turning the pages. She was in her stocking feet. Her high-heeled brown suede shoes were next to her on the floor. "You never showed me this," she said. It was a sketch of a group of people—a woman in a doorway, a seated woman, a man, a child.

"It was you at the door," I said. "You'd been here with Cynthia."

I'd drawn many such groups lately—two men and two women, two women and a man. Now a small publisher had requested drawings for a calendar, but they were to be of objects. I thought I'd draw bicycles or artichokes. I wanted things with many surfaces, like people.

Julie was putting her shoes on. She's a receptionist at a radio station. She'd come straight from work to pick up Cynthia, who had spent the afternoon with my daughter, Ann. I took the mugs and followed Julie downstairs. Her dress was brown, like the shoes, a warm brown with orange and gold designs in it. Her hair was very short, and as I walked behind her, I could see how it was cut to end in wisps at the nape of her neck, leaving bare the soft indentation between the bones at the base of her skull.

A few months ago, George had dinner at my house with Julie and Cynthia. After the meal, I came up behind him as he stood in the living room watching the girls, who were playing Scrabble on the floor.

"You didn't use the triple word Ann opened up," he said to Cynthia, who was leaning forward, one hand next to her on the rug, to make a word. George was blocking my view of the board.

"Where?" Cynthia said.

"There." He pointed with his foot.

"I didn't see it," she said. Then George's foot, in a black shoe, swung back and came down on Cynthia's outspread hand. She yelped, and George knelt and apologized. But a moment before, I had known it was going to happen, that George was about to step on Cynthia's hand.

Now Cynthia and Ann were in the basement. Julie called down the stairs. "Time to go, baby."

"In a second," came Cynthia's voice over the sound of women singing. I recognized the group—Sweet Honey in the Rock. I took the mugs into the kitchen. When I came back, Julie was in her jacket, standing near the front door. I could still hear music.

Julie looked at me. "Am I difficult?"

"No. Is that what he said?"

"I *am* difficult. I'm demanding."

"How are you going to forget him?"

"Keep busy, I guess," said Julie. "Isn't that the usual way? I'm working at the orchard on Saturday." The orchard is a few miles out of town—a farm stand that sells fruits and vegetables. Julie has worked there on occasional Saturdays for years. "The Liberty apples are in," she said. "My favorite. Tart but sweet."

"Could I draw them?" Fruit would be a good thing to draw, I thought.

"Oh—sure. Come Saturday. I'll sell apples, you draw them." She sounded more cheerful, but then she looked down, shook her head, and gave me a teary smile. "Stupid," she said. "I was remembering shopping at the farm with George." She found a tissue in her pocket. "It makes me feel married to a guy to shop with him. He kept saying 'we.' 'Do we need potatoes?' 'Should we get some honey?' Even though we didn't live together."

"It's good you've both decided to call it quits," I said. I couldn't seem to stop saying that. In fact it was only George who had decided.

"I know you think that," Julie said. "You think I'm better off."

"Of course you are."

Music was still coming from the basement, now a slow song. Julie glanced at her watch. "You're wrong about him," she said. She put her hand on the doorknob, then looked toward the basement door, but at last we heard feet on the stairs. "Look, I still love him," Julie said. "I'm not just letting it go."

I didn't answer.

"I might call him," Julie said.

"Don't."

"I might."

.

Julie gave me a Liberty apple as soon as I got to the farm stand on Saturday, and I ate it. "They're a cross between Macouns and an experimental apple with a name I forget," she said. "And we have fritters today, too. Did you ever taste them?"

"Apple fritters?" The fritters were big, glazed, lumpy ellipsoids kept in a Lucite box on the table in the middle of the barn, with a pair of tongs and a roll of plastic bags next to it.

I perched on a stool in the corner with my sketch pad. It was October, and the farm's bounty was before me: bushel baskets of apples, smaller bags of them— Liberty, Macoun, Jonathan, McIntosh, Golden Delicious, Red Delicious. There were brown pears. Along the side of the shed were baskets of eggplants, string beans, shell beans, broccoli, onions, and potatoes. Julie stood behind a counter on the other side, looking chilly, wearing a loose flannel shirt. She pulled the cuffs over her hands. The doorway was wide and I could see red and orange trees across the road, their branches moving when the wind blew.

"How are you?" I said.

"Better. Thanks for listening the other night." She sounded a bit distant.

"I *said* plenty, too."

"I'm glad you say what you think."

"I'm not apologizing," I said. Julie laughed shortly. A man and woman came in and chose pears, apples, and potatoes, calling suggestions to each other. They asked Julie about baking apples.

I sketched a basket of eggplants. They were small, and their shapes were luxurious. They had little green caps and stems.

The customers left. Julie glanced over her shoulder at the doorway. "I called him." She spread both hands, palm down, on the counter, leaning forward like an old-fashioned grocer in a commercial.

"Did you?" I was disappointed. "What happened?" I realized I wanted her to say George had hurt her, that it was a mistake to call.

"You were wrong," she said. "It was a good idea. It

cleared the air. And I really *had* to call—I remembered
that my camera is at his house."

My pencil moved faster because I was angry, and the
line I made was too dark and straight, not accurate.

"He said he'd let me know when was a good time to
come for it," Julie said.

"That's good," I managed to say. I was surprised at how
bad I felt. I wanted to take Julie's shoulders in my hands,
to pinch, even, if I had to. I wanted to get her attention.
I could hear a car pull up outside, then another.

For a while the stand was busy. I sketched shell beans.
A woman glanced at me, choosing some. "I'll get out of
your way in a minute."

"You're not in my way." I meant it, but I sounded
irritated. I was drawing rapidly. My hands were cold. The
beans were a dappled pink and white, like marble—there
was no way to convey the color. They were long, and they
intertwined. I tried to follow one with my eye and pencil,
then another. Then I quickly penciled in the long line of
the woman's open raincoat, the curve of her head, her
hand.

A voice I almost recognized passed my head like a gust
of rain from trees. ". . . in luck." I looked up. George
Friedman had come into the shed along with a woman in
a heavy white sweater. Now the woman was speaking quietly. Julie was adding up somebody's purchases. There
was a small manual cash register. When Julie depressed
the keys, numbers flew up, and there was a sharp ring.
She packed the fruit into a brown bag, then turned to
George. There were no other customers left.

"Hi," she said, and I thought that pain filled the air, as
if we had all plunged into a thicket of brambles.

"Julie, this is good luck," said George. He's a big man; he was dressed in a sport jacket and jeans. When he faced Julie, I could see the back of his head. He has thick, shaggy brown hair. "I didn't know whether you'd be here today."

"I'm here," said Julie.

"And I wasn't sure I could find it without you," he said. "This is Ingrid. You must have heard me talk about her. Ingrid and I go back—"

"Hi," said Julie, and Ingrid went to the counter and shook hands with her.

"Our mothers were friends," she said.

Ingrid had blond hair, which always makes me think a woman is young, but when I saw her face she seemed to be our age or older. Without thinking about it, I was drawing the group at the counter: Julie stretching her hand over it, Ingrid taking it, and George, standing nearest to me, the back of his sport coat a dark square near the women's heads.

"I've never seen you at work here," George was saying. "You look wise, as if you knew all about apples."

"I know a little," said Julie. The flannel shirt she was wearing—a bold blue plaid—was big on her, and her face looked small to me crowned with its cap of hair.

"You also know me," said George. "Which kind would I like?"

"I don't know." It was too much. George stepped away. Ingrid had turned to examine the vegetables and George joined her. They studied the broccoli and moved to the eggplants. Ingrid was saying something.

"Don't be silly," said George. Then he spotted me. "What are *you* doing here?"

"Working on some drawings," I said, closing my sketch pad and standing up. I introduced myself to Ingrid.

"We're figuring out what to cook tonight," she said. "I like eggplant."

George smiled at me, then turned and found the table of fritters. "Oh, *this* is what I want," he said. "I don't care about eggplant, Ingrid. Let's eat out. But here's dessert, or breakfast. We need fritters. Don't we need fritters?"

Ingrid examined the fritters in their clear plastic box. "Look," she said. "There are bees trapped inside."

"That doesn't matter," said George. "They're not dirty, like flies. They're yellow jackets, by the way, not bees. They're a variety of wasp. I'll let them out." He opened the box and stood with the cover in his hand.

"Be careful," said Ingrid. "They sting."

George took a plastic bag and began filling it with fritters, using the tongs. "Six?"

"We can't eat six."

"All right, four." They didn't buy vegetables, only a small bag of apples and the fritters. George advanced to the counter to pay. I sat down again. I concentrated on drawing a basket of potatoes, each one resting solidly on the layer below.

"If I'd been sure I was going to see you," George said to Julie, "I'd have brought your camera."

"It doesn't matter," said Julie. She stood looking at George as if she'd forgotten what her job required her to do next. "I guess we'll see each other."

"I can't imagine that we wouldn't," said George.

Ingrid joined them. "Such fine vegetables," she said, but then she stepped back and laughed. "Now there are bees in the bag of fritters."

"You're right," said Julie. She took the bag in her hands. George had tied the top closed and she began to work the knot loose.

I dropped my pencil and sketch pad and stepped forward. I've drawn Julie's hands more than once and I knew how they looked up close. She has long, narrow hands that look more knowing than her face. They are beautiful. I felt that they must not be stung. I had to push George aside to reach the counter. I took the bag. There were the wasps, moving a little inside. Julie stepped back, smiling faintly, while I brought a second plastic bag and the tongs from the table. Then I opened the knot. There were four yellow jackets here and there on the fritters, their plump striped bodies quivering. I used the tongs to take each fritter out and place it in the second bag. The yellow jackets stayed in the first bag.

"Now what are we going to do with these fellows?" said George as I tied the new bag closed and laid it on the counter.

"I'll just carry them outside," said Ingrid. George was counting out dollar bills. Julie dropped his change into his hand, then stuck her hand in her pocket. Ingrid grasped the bag of wasps at the top, carried it out of the barn, and knelt on the ground just outside. I was waiting to be alone with Julie, to step behind the counter and put my arms around her. Ingrid unfolded the top of the bag and laid it down, watching until the four yellow jackets flew out one at a time, buzzed in circles, and disappeared.

RAYMOND

&

LEONA

George's parents, in their seventies, told stories of hearty people in their nineties—a woman they knew who'd taken a lover, a man who lectured on Caravaggio to their Elder Hostel class. "His body was not what it should be," said George's mother to Ingrid. "I can't deny that. But his mind!"

They didn't want to hear about Ingrid's mother, who had died a few months before at only sixty-nine, though Mrs. Friedman had known her all her life. "She was my little sister," she said, suddenly addressing the subject after all—her voice lowered—and taking Ingrid's hand in hers when they all (Mr. and Mrs. Friedman, Ingrid, and George) stood to go into the breakfast room for lunch. "She was like a sister to me. I walked her to school when she was in second grade and I was in fourth." Her hand was firm and large, not frail, and Ingrid, giddy with jet lag, felt tears well up, though she thought severely that at the moment she was *not* mourning Mother (she'd become an expert, these months, in differentiating among tears). She was just feeling a rush of relief to be young again.

Ingrid's father had died years earlier, and Ingrid had felt old since her mother died—the next to go. Here in the living room of her old friend's—old lover's—parents in New Haven, Connecticut, with the reds and oranges of autumn outside and George's mother taking her hand to lead her to lunch (as she had led Ingrid's mother, all those years ago, to the second grade), Ingrid felt young—*younger* than young: a generation younger, after all, than the enterprising youngsters about to feed her cheese from their authentic Italian market and bread from the bakery only they knew about, this sprightly couple already arguing about which Elder Hostel course to take next, Jazz or Jane Austen. Ingrid had never heard of Elder Hostels and didn't know if they existed in California, where she lived. She knew about hospitals, nursing homes, hospices. George's father had impatiently tossed brochures in her lap. Weeklong programs, he explained, for seniors, at colleges. The friends they'd made, the strange accommodations they'd put up with! "In Vermont," he said, "Lilly had to shower in the men's bathroom. The shower in the ladies' was out of order."

"Who cares?" said Lilly Friedman. "I kept hoping I'd see something good."

Ingrid had always liked the Friedmans and was sorry she hadn't gotten them for in-laws, except that she'd have had to marry George. None of them had ever married, in fact—not she, not George, not Pippin, the third member of the trio of friends that had formed twenty years ago when Ingrid's mother persuaded Ingrid, a freshman at the University of Michigan, to look up her old friend Lilly's son, then a junior. When Ingrid found out George's room number, marched into his dorm, and knocked on his door, her roommate, Pippin, was at her side for courage.

They were still a trio, though Ingrid had seen little of Pippin or George in the last years. Ingrid was a lawyer in a firm in San Francisco that did a lot of pro bono work and assigned her mostly to environmental cases. For ten years now, she'd had a married lover, and unlike many of her friends who'd tried that, she was happy with the arrangement. She liked living alone and she knew exactly when she'd see Howard, who was predictable—visible at certain hours of the week, invisible at others—and who, when he was angry with her, didn't express it by disappearing. But it had given her terrible pain that her mother had happened to die on a Wednesday, when she never saw or spoke to him.

Ingrid hadn't married and neither had George, whose lovers lasted for a year or two and were rapidly succeeded by others, nor had Pippin until now. She seemed the type to marry right out of college, but had hardly had any men in her life until a couple of years ago, when she'd met a systems engineer named Ron. She was marrying him the next day in a Boston suburb. Ingrid had flown into Hartford on Friday night, spent the night on the sofa at George's, and was spending the day with him in New Haven, where he had been born and grown up and had always lived, except for college. The next day they'd drive to the wedding, and afterward George would take her to Logan Airport. She'd be back in California Monday morning.

Lilly heaped Ingrid's plate with salad, and Mr. Friedman passed her the long loaf of crusty bread. "Take a big piece," he said. "It's good. Though I didn't bake it myself."

"Can you bake bread?" said Ingrid.

"I've made a few loaves," he said. "When I retired, I needed activities. I like to look under the towel and see how the dough is twice as big as it was."

"Like watching the stock market go up," said George.

"Better," said his father.

"Or a penis," whispered Lilly to Ingrid, passing her a bowl of black olives.

George snorted, though he hadn't heard his mother, Ingrid saw; he was snorting at his father, his familiar snort, almost a whinny, which she remembered from the first weeks she'd known him, when she had flinched if George whinnied at her—and he did, for thinking Julie Andrews was good in *Mary Poppins,* for making her bed every day. His father didn't seem to notice the snort, though he turned toward George now. "If you had a few more satisfying interests," he said, "like baking bread, maybe you wouldn't be so restless with the ladies. Lilly tells me you and Julie are having problems."

"Unfortunately, yes," said George. "I expected too much of her."

Ingrid had been hearing about Julie for a while. She hadn't heard about problems.

"I was hoping you'd marry her," said Mr. Friedman.

George, helping himself to cheese, shook his head as if answering his father was not worth the trouble, but his mother spoke up. "I disagree completely," she said. "I like Julie, except I think she's timid. But what's so special about marriage?" She turned to her husband. "Why do

179

young people feel this pressure to marry?" Now she looked
at Ingrid. "I admire you—all three of you. Well, Pippin
is getting married, but I admire her for waiting until the
time was right. And I admire you in particular, Ingrid."
She stopped to chew, and Ingrid wondered whether Mrs.
Friedman knew about Howard, her lover. She didn't think
her mother or George would have mentioned him—and so
it appeared. "I admire your independence," Lilly was saying. "Relying on your work and friendships for richness
and—and everything else life has to offer. Not being de-
pendent on men and babies. Your mother wrote me about
some of the cases you've worked on. Those fishermen! I
think you have a wonderful life."

Fishermen. Ingrid took a moment, then realized that
Lilly Friedman meant a case she'd argued against a large
company that processed fish for frozen fish sticks. They
had been doing business with fishermen who used harmful
nets, but the fishermen themselves had been far from Ingrid. She listened, eating her lunch in the sunny breakfast
room, and was suddenly filled with sorrow for herself. If
she'd even known any of those fishermen! Why, here was
Pippin, hinting about having a baby. At her age it would
take years to become pregnant. And George, breaking up
with still another woman. As for Ingrid, what if she died,
someday, on a Wednesday, when Howard wouldn't know
and couldn't come?

.

"I have a few errands," said George, as they drove away
from his parents' house. Ingrid didn't answer. The Friedmans had given her a headache. In a friendlier voice,

George said, "What shall we do—eventually—about dinner?"

Ingrid said she'd cook. "I've been eating a lot of vegetables lately," she said, "but I don't mind meat. I'll cook whatever you feel like." She would like cooking in George's kitchen.

"Oh, vegetables," said George. "I know just the place for vegetables."

"Eggplant," said Ingrid. She would live, she decided, for the little things—the color of eggplant, the smell of garlic. Then, "Do you regret your life?" she asked boldly.

George didn't snort as she expected—he laughed. "Does that mean I'm about to die?" he said. "Did you come east to kill me at long last?"

"No."

"It would be hard on my parents."

"Oh, I don't know—they wouldn't have to worry about your women anymore."

"But still . . ."

"Well, I'm not going to kill you."

"Good," he said. "Boy, I haven't thought *that* in a long time. I used to imagine that you and Pippin would do it together."

Ingrid laughed. "I suppose there were times when we were tempted."

Clearly George didn't want to discuss whether or not he regretted his life. Maybe he didn't regret it. His job was good: he was an investment banker. As for women, he didn't seem to notice the length of the series. Each one was going to work out until she didn't. Ingrid and George would phone each other every few months, and in every other call, he seemed to have a new woman to tell her about—the intricacies of getting together. The calls in between were about the intricacies of breaking up.

George stopped at a dry cleaner's and Ingrid waited in the car until he came out with a few cleaner's plastic bags, on hangers, streaming behind him. She was down the street, and she watched him come nearer, holding his clothes on his shoulder, a jaunty large man in a tweed jacket and blue jeans. His hair was still thick, not gray at all. She often felt that she'd failed with George, as if he were her child. He'd been difficult when she and Pippin met him. He had few friends—maybe that was why he was so eager to join up with a pair of girl freshmen. She had thought they would teach him to act like a nicer person. She knew that he was one underneath. But when he talked about his girlfriends, still, though he had the perceptiveness of a woman, a woman's interest in getting the nuances clear, he revealed himself, over and over again, as—well, a jerk. She hadn't known he was breaking up with Julie and she didn't know whether he'd done anything bad to her yet.

The next errands were also fast: a restrung tennis racket to be retrieved and a stop at a drugstore for extra-strong dandruff shampoo. She went into the drugstore with George, and they walked up and down the aisles. He picked up some toothpaste as well, and contact lens wetting solution.

"I don't like you to see that I need this shampoo," he said as they waited on the checkout line. "I'm as vain as ever."

"I don't think of you as vain, exactly," she said.

"But I'm arrogant," he said promptly, and she laughed,

because that was exactly what he was, but she had never known that he knew it. *Arrogant* hadn't been her and Pippin's word for it, though, and as George paid for his purchases she tried to remember what it was they had said. *Conceited.* He probably told all his women he was arrogant. *That* would be disarming—and sure enough, none of them had killed him yet.

"Now for the vegetables," George said. "I know the perfect place." It was a farm stand out of town along a suburban road, just where it became country. The ride in the autumn colors cheered Ingrid. "I'm arrogant, it's true," George said again. "I feel bad about Julie. Perfectly nice, but the nicer they are, the less I want them."

"I wonder why that is," said Ingrid.

"Who knows," he said, not making it a question.

"What does she do?"

"She works at the radio station." He'd been doing a show on the radio for a year or so—a ten-minute talk once a week about savings and investments. He'd sent Ingrid a tape and she'd found the contents boring, but had liked the liveliness of George's voice.

"What does she look like?"

George didn't answer. He was parking the car in front of a barn. Ingrid was charmed. It was just the sort of place she would have chosen to visit on this brief trip east. Signs advertised cider and doughnuts, tomatoes and apples. Within the barn, she could see them arrayed on tables and in crates. She and George climbed out of the car and walked a few yards to the doorway.

"You want to find out?" he said.

"Find out what?" said Ingrid. She'd forgotten her question.

"What Julie looks like."

"What do you mean?"

"Well, I said she works at the radio station, and she does," he said. "But for extra money, on Saturdays she's sometimes the cashier here." By now they had both stepped through the wide door into the dimness of the barn. "We're in luck," said George in a low voice. "There she is."

.

Pippin was short and chubby with little round breasts, which she displayed without self-consciousness. Ingrid, as a freshman, had found undressing in front of her roommate as new and unsettling as she found her math professor, who spoke with a foreign accent and didn't try to learn anyone's name, or her English professor, who used the word *fucking*, though not about sex. ("A fucking reactionary," he said about someone.) Pippin would go out into the hall to take a phone call stark naked.

Ingrid, on the other hand, was less cowed than Pippin by George, even though it was hard for her to knock on his door that first time. The young man who answered looked Ingrid and Pippin over curiously, not inviting them in until they'd managed to explain themselves. They weren't too clear about it. George had heavy black-rimmed glasses and he looked soberly through them while Ingrid explained about her mother, Sigrid Larsen, who was his mother's friend. At last he remembered, or decided there *might* be such a person. "Sorry to be so dense," he said, as they came in and sat down. "The bores around here. I wouldn't want to get into some kind of obligation thing with them."

Ingrid wanted to say that of course there was no obligation, but Pippin agreed about the bores. Before the end of the week, the three of them had a code. They'd sit in the Student Union drinking Cokes and watching people go by, or talking about people they knew. Some people— George's roommate, for example—were Harmless And Lovable Fatheads. "Oh, he's a HALF," any of the three of them would say to another. A DOUBLE meant a Disgusting Or Utterly Boring Limited Entity. The worst was a TRIPLE—a Truly Rotten Individual, Past Logical Expectations. People they liked were called Zips, which didn't break up into anything. They didn't come across too many Zips.

Just after midterms in the spring term, when they'd been friends for three or four months, Ingrid discovered that Pippin and George were sleeping together. He told her himself. It was a warmish day and she was feeling depressed and lonely, not knowing why, although when she thought about it later, she realized that there had been many times lately when Pippin had said she needed to study alone in the library and George had said *he* needed to study alone in his room. Ingrid hadn't done very well on her midterms. She had worked fitfully, alone in her room, waiting for Pippin. Now she and George went for a long walk in the newly warm weather and got thoroughly chilled, because it wasn't *that* warm. Half a mile into it, George said, "I have to tell you something. Don't tell Pippin I told you."

And he told her. Ingrid felt left out, and stupid not to have guessed, and ugly not to have been chosen. She walked with her head down, the warm wind blowing under her hat and making her ears ache. Her hands were in her pockets. After a while, George drew one hand out, and then instead of taking it he put his arm around her and pulled her close to him. "I have another confession to make," he said. "This gets worse and worse"—but he sounded a little excited, and Ingrid began to take heart. "I think I picked the wrong roommate."

That day was the first time Ingrid slept with George. Later she was a mess—angry, happy, guilty, startled at the blood (she'd been a virgin), though of course she'd known about the blood. She fell in love with George instantly and life was hard for the next few weeks, during which Pippin sometimes left the room to study, though not as often, and Ingrid and George furtively made love twice more. When they were all three together, there was so much tense laughter that Ingrid's face would hurt later and she could not sleep. At last Pippin told her she'd met a guy, a sophomore named Joe, and then they had it out. Pippin had known almost all along, it turned out. She'd felt hurt, too. They both cried and hugged, standing in the middle of their room, with Ingrid, who was tall, resting her head tenderly on Pippin's. For a few days they were inseparable and avoided both men. Then Ingrid began to see George openly—it lasted for six months or so, but they slept together less and less often—and they sometimes did things as a foursome with Pippin and Joe. By the middle of sophomore year, though—George's senior year—they were back where they'd begun: Joe was forgotten and they were always together, always a trio, always dismissing something or someone—a book, a rule, a professor, a friend.

Walks became one of their things, and they took walks even in the winter, even with hard snow blowing in their faces. They continued in spring. Just before exams, just before they were all going to separate for the summer and, as far as George was concerned, possibly for life, they walked one night, after seeing *Jules et Jim,* from the campus to downtown Ann Arbor and then on into a residential neighborhood. They were quiet. The air was soft and warm, breezy. Ingrid had borrowed a sweater of Pippin's when they started to walk—Ingrid was chilly and Pippin wasn't—and she was wearing it buttoned up. It was tight on her and made her feel sexy, and it was white, a color she didn't usually wear, but which she found she liked. From now on, she told herself, she'd wear white. It was a risky, interesting color, to her surprise. A blonde, she'd always thought white made her look angelic—sappy.

Then Pippin said, "Every person in these houses is a HALF, a DOUBLE, or a TRIPLE." They laughed. They'd forgotten their old code.

"I know," said George. "I can't stand it. You two are so lucky, you've got two more years. Here I'm graduating— I'm supposed to *join* these creeps?" He was thinking of business school, but hadn't applied. He said he'd go home to New Haven and look for a job.

"I wonder which house has the creepiest people," said Ingrid.

For a while they tried to decide. They stopped in the dark in front of each house and analyzed it. What they liked was evidence of individuality, of complexity—maybe an ancient car in the driveway, meticulously kept up, or even the lack of a paint job. "We're not intellectual snobs," Pippin defended them. "It's not that they have to have books you can see through the window." It was hard to see anything in windows. Everything was dark. It was after two in the morning.

Then George said, "I think this is the neighborhood where I used to break into houses."

Pippin laughed shortly, but something stirred in Ingrid's stomach. "Where you did *what*?"

"Before I knew you," he said, after a pause. The pause made Ingrid know he was telling the truth. If he'd been making it up, it would have come more easily. "My sophomore year," he said. "I used to take long walks at night, all by myself, and in the spring, I noticed that people left their houses open—a window would be open on the porch, or you could just slide it up. So I'd pick one and make sure there was no dog and no TV on—some insomniac, you know, whiling away the hours—and I'd go inside."

"Did you take things?" said Pippin, her voice a little hushed.

"Not always. Sometimes I'd just stand there for a while or walk through the rooms on the first floor. Sometimes I'd take something—something like a box of cookies. Once I took a briefcase. That's where I got that leather briefcase."

He did use a leather briefcase to carry books and papers to class or to the library. It made him stand out—no one else did that.

"I don't believe it," said Pippin. "I don't believe you broke into houses."

"Have I ever lied to you?"

Ingrid believed him. George was full of puzzles and pretense, but this was different. His voice was different. "So you want to break in someplace now?" she said. She said it slowly and soberly, so they would know she meant it. She wasn't sure why she wanted to do it. It seemed easy—the night was warm, windows were open, it was almost as if the outdoor and indoor spaces blended, and the people in the houses were already *with* them. Walking past one house, she'd heard someone snoring. But also, there was a kind of insolence about the darkened houses. She wanted to show them up, prove something to them, or disprove something the houses believed was true.

"Sure," said George. Pippin was less certain, but they walked around for another hour, and she couldn't let the idea go. It was she who kept bringing it up again when George or Ingrid changed the subject. "So—we could really do it? We could just break in somewhere?" And it was Pippin who thought up the little twist that made it interesting. "Let's steal something," she said, "but not something valuable, and not just cookies. Let's steal something these people need to—to keep on leading their stupid little lives. So they'll *change*."

"Being stupid isn't their fault," said Ingrid.

"Their vacant lives. Their empty lives. Let's each take something," Pippin said. "I'm going to take the *TV Guide*."

They picked out a small dark house without distinguishing characteristics. There was no stroller on the porch signaling a baby who might wake and cry. When they approached, no dog barked. They circled the house, and George pointed out a window in the back. Garbage cans were lined up under it, and he climbed onto one while Ingrid held the lid down so it wouldn't clank. He raised the window, which went up quickly. The storm window must have been up because of the warm weather, but there was no screen. The people hadn't put it in yet. George climbed inside, then leaned out. "It's a kitchen counter," he whispered. "Don't knock anything off it. Now we all go in, and we all come back in *one minute*—with something." He paused. "With an *artifact*."

Pippin and then Ingrid climbed onto the garbage can and through the window. The kitchen still smelled of last night's dinner—a dank smell, as if these people cooked vegetables for too long. Smelling it was like catching a glimpse of someone's slip when she went upstairs. There were canisters lined up on the counter—Flour, Sugar, Coffee, Tea—and Ingrid thought one of them might do as her artifact, but it seemed like cheating not to venture farther in. She let herself off the counter carefully. She could see a little—a streetlight shone in a side window. In front of her was a table with a newspaper on it. She recognized the headline she'd seen on newsstands all day.

Pippin and George had left the kitchen. There was a long hallway, and Ingrid walked down it toward the front door. She knew she mustn't open the door and run away. She didn't see Pippin and George. Next to the hallway were a living room and dining room, and her friends had to be in there. On the other side of the hall was a staircase. In the hall beside her was a small wooden table with a telephone on it.

She heard a sound. She was sure it was George or Pippin, but she was afraid. Beside the telephone on the little table was an address book with a red leatherette cover, and Ingrid swiftly picked it up and fled to the kitchen. George was crouched on the counter, and he pointed silently out the window to show that Pippin had gone out already. He vaulted through the window, and then Ingrid climbed onto the counter and followed him. She was afraid to turn her head in case one of the residents had heard them and come into the room. She managed to close the window and dropped from the garbage can to the driveway. Then they all walked quickly and quietly away from the house. They didn't talk for a block. Pippin was holding her arms folded across her breasts—it seemed to have turned cold while they were inside—but didn't think to ask for the sweater. She had been unable to find the *TV Guide* but had stolen a box of Rice-a-Roni from the pantry, which she insisted was even better. George had a vase of plastic flowers.

Ingrid felt bad about the address book, which she kept for years. It wasn't a cultural artifact, the others pointed out immediately, it was just a thing. And doing without it must have been a terrible nuisance to the people in the house. It was a well-used address book, with many names and addresses and telephone numbers in different colors of ink. Every now and then Ingrid read it from front to back. After the first few months she lost the intense unease she felt about it and found it comforting. She sometimes wished she could return it, but the residents had not written their own name and address at the front of the book, and she had no idea where the house was. The handwriting— a woman's—was like her mother's, and some names in the book were ones Ingrid associated with an older genera- tion. Ingrid decided the owners were an elderly couple. "Edna and Bill Flynn" was one entry, in Kansas City. Edna seemed like an old-fashioned name. Ingrid con- sidered sending the book to the Flynns, or to one of the other couples listed in it (the people who owned the book seemed to know only couples). But she thought the Flynns wouldn't know who it belonged to either. They'd be people met up with on a bus tour, Ingrid decided, never seen again. The people closest to the owners were doubtless those designated only by first names, often in pencil, with no address, just a local phone number. "Raymond & Leona"—with an ampersand—was one such pair, under

P, for a last name that was so familiar it didn't have to be written down. Ingrid knew that if she were to call Leona, together they could figure out who owned the address book. "Let's see," Leona would say. "Do they know the Wheelers? Look under W, honey, and see if it says Mary and Mike. It does? Then it has to be—"

But of course Ingrid could never call Leona. Ingrid was a criminal. She had stolen this book, and she didn't have the nerve to pretend to Leona that she'd found it. After a few years she thought it was too late, anyway. Raymond and Leona might have moved or died or changed their number because of crank calls. Ingrid kept the book all through law school and beyond, looking through it every so often, thinking about the unnamed people who owned it, the named people it seemed to honor, and the life, which she had scorned and invaded, around the little table.

.

The old woman sitting next to Ingrid at Pippin's wedding reception couldn't get it straight about Ingrid and George. She assumed they were married when Ingrid began to tell her about George's parents' experiences at Elder Hostels. The old woman had tried one once but disliked the food. "I'm spoiled," she said. "I like foreign places where they give you herring in wine sauce for breakfast. Next summer I'm going on a cruise to Spitzbergen. Polar bears."

Her husband, she said, nodding in George's direction, had been dead for decades, but she wasn't going to stay home and weep. She was alone at the wedding, and Ingrid liked talking to her. Otherwise she felt a little off balance. Pippin was in full bride's regalia, including a train, but it wasn't just that Ingrid was afraid she'd trip on her old friend when she tried to hug her. She'd forgotten, somehow, that at a wedding Pippin would have a husband, and there he was, Ron—whom Ingrid had never met—a jocund, bald man with engaging sloppiness: right now he looked sloppy in a tuxedo. He had two daughters from his first marriage, and there *they* were, and two brothers—at least—and innumerable aunts, uncles, and others. He had always lived near Boston, Ingrid recalled. Pippin, who was from Cincinnati and came from a family of small families, had produced, for this occasion, only Ingrid and George, some newer friends, and her parents, shy people who always seemed to be stepping backward when Ingrid caught sight of them at this reception—stepping out of a waiter's way, or stepping back so as not to be stepped on or splattered by one of Ron's relatives, or simply moving backward: as she finished her fruit cup, Ingrid had looked up and seen Pippin's mother backing up into a fold of one of the dark-red velvet curtains that lined the walls of the room.

Ingrid couldn't figure out her new friend, the old woman, any more than the woman could figure her out. Their table seemed to be for friends, but surely the woman was a relative; surely she'd heard Ron call her Aunt Laura. "Are you Ron's aunt?" she asked, finally.

"No, I'm *Louisa's* aunt," said Aunt Laura a little mischievously. "Ron's first wife. I'm close to both of them. Not that they aren't still close to each other. An amicable divorce."

"How nice!" said Ingrid brightly. "Louisa's not here, is she?"

"They considered it," said Aunt Laura. "But no, she's not. They thought it would be confusing for the children."

The children looked about seven and ten. Ingrid remembered that Pippin was wary of them. She wanted to talk to Pippin—who, after all, was the person she knew here aside from George, who was easily making friends with everyone at their table. Ingrid had eaten all the chicken she wanted, she decided. Dancing had begun, and she saw that Ron was now dancing with a gray-haired woman who surely *was* his aunt. George was dancing with the woman who'd been sitting on his other side, and Pippin was alone. Ingrid stood up and made her way to the bridal table, pushed aside some of Pippin's white yardage, and sat down next to her.

"You and George look like a couple," said Pippin. They'd already greeted each other on the receiving line. They'd stood there and laughed, as though they knew something about this gathering unknown to anyone else.

"Apparently," said Ingrid. "Pip, that woman is Ron's first wife's aunt."

"Aunt Laura," said Pippin. "I put her next to you on purpose. She's a character."

"Does it bother you that she's connected to Louisa?"

"I like her. I like Louisa, too. I *need* Louisa. She gives me advice about the kids. So how's our George?"

"Hasn't changed," said Ingrid. "Have you heard about Julie?"

"Who's Julie?"

"A woman George just broke up with. He took me to meet her yesterday."

"Why?" Ingrid told her about the farm stand. They'd gone in, and there had been Julie, looking, she told Pippin, as if she had an unusually fragile heart. "She was selling apples."

"Did she think you and George were lovers?"

"I suppose so. I don't know *what* she thought."

"And George did this on purpose so she'd think that?"

"Quite possibly."

"Couldn't you tell her?" Pippin said.

"I couldn't, I was so startled. I didn't know how. Also, I didn't like her enough to," Ingrid said. "Why do people take up with him? Didn't she have any sense?"

"*We* took up with him."

"We were nineteen. This woman was our age. Our present age."

"Don't remind me," said Pippin. "Don't remind me of our present age. Did you get enough to eat?"

"I'm fine," said Ingrid. "It's a nice wedding. All these relatives—it's like you called up central casting and said, 'Send me a wedding.' "

"I know it. That's how I feel, and now they're mine."

The music stopped. George's partner went back to the table and he came over to Ingrid and Pippin. "It's hot in here," he said.

"Let's go for a walk," said Pippin. Ingrid looked around. They were in a motel ballroom, the sort of indoor place that doesn't seem connected to the outdoors. But she supposed the world was out there. They'd come on a highway, but there might be streets, a town. There were no windows—but there were the dark-red velvet drapes. Perhaps there were windows behind them.

"A walk in that getup?" she said.

"I don't care. It has to go to the dry cleaner's whatever I do—it's not as though if I'm careful, I can wear it tomorrow."

"I suppose not." The music had started up again. Ingrid thought they'd be mobbed if they stood up—Pippin was like a float in a parade, a cynosure. But no one seemed to notice. Ron was dancing with one of the daughters. "That's Alexandra," said Pippin, as they stood and scanned the dance floor. "She's the younger one. She wets the bed, but she's my buddy." They began to move toward a doorway. Even the bride, Ingrid considered, was probably allowed to go to the ladies' room. "The other daughter," said Pippin, "is Jackie. Jackie isn't sure about me yet, but we're working on it. She's a gymnast. She studies gymnastics. At first she was usually mad at me because I kept calling it tumbling."

"Do you have a coat?" said George. Pippin didn't, but it wasn't very cold out. They saw a red-lit exit sign at the end of the corridor, past the rest rooms, and stepped out into the parking lot. Pippin had taken off her train and thrown her veil back over her head. Now she gathered the skirts of her dress in one hand, but she still looked more like a symbol than a person, Ingrid thought, as they zigzagged among the cars to the edge of the parking lot.

She herself was in a long-sleeved blue silk dress, and she was cold. She had a coat, but it was in a cloakroom down a different corridor, near the main entrance of the building. She'd left her purse at the table. It was a crisp, bright October day, and the wind cut through her dress, but she didn't mind. It was a relief to be out. It had been hot inside—and there didn't seem to be enough air there.

At the edge of the parking lot was a woods, and disappearing into the woods was a path, a level, dry-looking path that even Ingrid and Pippin, in their high-heeled shoes, could walk on. They stepped out of the parking lot and in under the trees, where the sunshine was dimmed and there was a slight sound of dry leaves rattling together and falling.

It was a real woods, though not a large one. In the distance, beyond the red and brown trees, Ingrid could see a highway. "This is the sort of place where they find bodies," said George as they walked, Pippin going last, clutching her skirts, crushing dry leaves under her feet. "A wooded area. 'The body was discovered in a wooded area behind the motel.' "

"Whose body?" called Pippin.

"Oh, anybody's body. Any body at all."

The path was descending, and they saw that it led to a pond, a shallow pond with mud around it and some beer cans—and yet a pond, with grasses at its edge and logs here and there that stretched into the water. The three of them stood in a row just above the pond, looking at it together, looking for a long time, as if there were much to see. Across the pond, a red tree was reflected. Pippin stood between Ingrid and George, and they might have been posing for a portrait, they stood so still.

Then Ingrid saw a turtle. "Look!" she cried, and Pippin pulled her skirts higher, around her knees, as if one of the bodies George had mentioned had turned up. "There!"

It was a large turtle sunning itself on a rock. They watched it.

"Look how it stretches its neck," Ingrid said.

"I wonder if it has a mate around somewhere," said Pippin.

"No, it's a loner," George said. "I recognize its air of independence."

"Or loneliness," said Ingrid.

"Creative solitude," George said, and the turtle abruptly dove and disappeared. Ripples spread around it, and when the widest one reached the shore with a small sound, they all turned and went back along the path.

"I suppose I ought to be at my wedding," said Pippin.

"And it's chilly," Ingrid said.

They emerged into the parking lot and Pippin let her skirts billow out around her, shaking the wrinkles out of them. Ingrid bent down and plucked two dry leaves off Pippin's hem. They crossed the lot. They found the inconspicuous door by which they'd come out, but it was locked. They hadn't thought of that.

"Well, if they don't *want* us," said George, and instead of circling the building to find the main entrance, they strolled up and down in a driveway next to it, until George thought to step over a curb and a strip of gravel outside the windows of the building. Inside were red draperies, and Ingrid realized they were outside the room where the wedding reception was taking place. George put his hands to the glass, shading his eyes, and looked in. Then he moved farther along to another place. Then a third. "There's a space between the drapes," he said. "Look. We can see into Pippin's wedding."

He made room for Pippin, who crouched down a little so the two of them could look at once. "How funny," she said. "There's Ron talking to someone. I don't know who he is. There's his mother. There's *my* mother. Oh, look, they're bringing in the wedding cake."

She moved aside so Ingrid could see. She didn't seem to be in any hurry. Ingrid put up her own hands and watched. It was like being at a play. Nobody could see her, nobody paid her any attention, yet all over the room there were things to look at: couples talking, people drinking, children running. A little girl—the older daughter, what was her name? Jackie—Jackie suddenly began doing cartwheels. She was wearing a short dark dress and its skirt flopped over as she turned. She had white tights on. Two elderly women were in her way. They didn't seem to notice her. She stood up, walked to a clearer space, and began again. Now Jackie turned cartwheel after cartwheel without a pause. Nobody turned, either to stop her or to applaud. Maybe they were used to her. Then Ingrid saw the wedding photographer notice the little girl whose hair flew out as she turned over and over. He shifted his camera, knelt on one knee, and began to shoot.

STRAWBERRIES

My daughter, Leah, once said she felt upset but she didn't know why, and I told her about the beginning of *The Merchant of Venice:* Antonio comes onto the stage, *before* his troubles begin, and says, "In sooth, I know not why I am so sad."

"It happens," I said to her.

Occasionally she would say "sooth," after that, to tell me she felt that unreasonable sadness, and she said it barefoot on a morning in June when the sun came through the partly opened venetian blinds in our kitchen and striped her white night-gown with brighter white. It was about nine, and I'd had breakfast. My brother was coming to visit, so I'd washed and put away my dish, because he comments on what he sees. He'd want to know what I eat for breakfast, why I use a plate, not a bowl.

"Did you just wake up?" I said.

"No, I've been lying in bed." She rested her hand lightly on the doorknob of the big closet we have in our kitchen, and began to do pliés and relevés in first and second position. I split an English muffin for her, toasted and buttered it, and poured some juice.

"The Japanese army," said Leah, still for a moment. "Were they volunteers?"

"In World War Two? I don't know."

"We saw a movie in Social Studies," she said. She'd just finished seventh grade. "The men who flew planes into tanks—"

"Oh, the kamikaze pilots," I said. "Oh, yes, I think they were volunteers."

"They were *happy*," she said. "And then they took off and slammed into the tanks."

I felt lonely, watching her do pliés again, unable to see the image in her mind, not even knowing whether the planes she would see whenever the subject came up crossed the screen from the right or the left.

"Come and eat," I said. But just then the doorbell rang. I went to answer it, angry with my brother, Gilbert, for coming so early, but it was my friend Elaine instead.

"I brought you strawberries," said Elaine. "The kids and I went to a place where you pick your own." She followed me back into the kitchen, carefully holding a big flat box of strawberries. She was wearing a yellow tank top with her jeans, and she plucked the long sleeve of my blue sweatshirt and laughed—I'm always cold and she's always hot.

"They're gorgeous," I said, taking the box and putting it on the table. "What will I do with so many?"

"Look, you don't have to come this afternoon," she said.

"Why not?" Elaine's kids were about to visit her ex-husband for the first time, by plane—they were probably downstairs in the car on their way to the airport. Elaine expected to feel bad, so we'd planned to spend the afternoon together. I'd told Gilbert he'd have to leave early and arranged for Leah to visit a friend.

"Where's Leah?" said Elaine. She wasn't in the room.

"Getting dressed, I suppose."

Elaine glanced toward the doorway. "I ought to put in some time at the office this weekend."

But I can read her. "It's a guy, isn't it?" I said. "The one you mentioned. Does he come in on Saturdays?"

"I'm sorry," she said. "Does it make you angry? It should."

"Yes." But we'd dealt with worse. Now the doorbell rang again, and this time it *was* Gilbert. He and Elaine said hello, and she rushed off, leaving Gilbert and me in the kitchen, where he stood smiling at me, patting the nearest thing—a chair back—with his hand.

Gilbert is forty-four, nine years older than I am. His hands are long and narrow. They look as if he could fold them lengthwise. His hair has been a little grayer each year; that day I noticed it was speckled all over. "You and I are all we have," Gilbert says to me annually when he calls, the third week of June (I'm supposed to remember that this will happen and be expecting his call, but I never am), to say he's thirty miles away, visiting his wife's parents, and wants to spend Saturday with me. He means we have no other brothers or sisters, and our parents are dead.

Now he sat down at the kitchen table, not where Leah's muffin was, but in front of the strawberries. He glanced at the muffin. "Leah's getting dressed," I said.

"I can't wait to see her."

I was happy to see him, as it turned out. Gilbert remembered he hadn't kissed me—because Elaine had been there—and so he stood up and did it now, laughing a little. He has a long sloping nose and he looked around like a fine-snouted sensitive gray dog sniffing out the events of the time he'd missed. He spotted a poster Leah had made hanging on the bulletin board. "Recycle Trash," it said, with a crossed-out picture of a garbage can. "Oh, are you big on recycling lately?"

"What?" The poster was months old, and I'd stopped seeing it. "Leah did it for school."

Then Gilbert wanted to know where I'd gotten so many strawberries. "Can you use them before they spoil?" I said Elaine had brought them, and he asked how I knew her. I didn't tell him she was the reason he had to leave early, nor that she'd canceled, so I was now free to spend the afternoon with him. I thought maybe I'd tell him later.

"You look like Dad," I said instead.

"May I eat some of these?" He reached for the strawberries.

Our father died five years ago. It was the way Gilbert's hair was cut that reminded me, or the way the hair fell on his head. I remembered how the side of my father's head felt—pleasantly rough, with short hair near his ears and longer, smoother hair higher up—and Gilbert's head looked as if it would feel the same way. I offered him coffee (he was eating strawberries and making a little pile of the hulls) and put the pot on the stove. Then I set out mugs and spoons and filled the creamer. The sugar bowl was empty, and so I put it down on the table and went to the big closet—it's almost a pantry—where I keep sugar.

"Why don't we talk more, Amy?" Gilbert asked, as my hand was on the doorknob. I didn't know whether he meant we should talk on the phone more often, or talk—right then—more openly or intensely. I stopped, embarrassed, and shrugged like a child. Then I opened the closet.

"Oh!" I said, because Leah was standing inside it in her nightgown, but she gave me a look of such misery that I stepped in beside her and pulled the door closed. Gilbert had his back to it.

She was frantically shushing me. "What are you doing here?" I whispered. "Have you been in here all along?"

"I don't want anyone to see me in my nightgown," whispered Leah. "Pretend I'm not here. *Please.*"

"I can't," I said. "Shall I get your bathrobe?"

"No. *Please.* No."

There was silence from outside the closet.

"I'll take him into the living room," I said, patting her shoulder. "Then you go get dressed." There wasn't room for both of us between the shelves and the door, and so we were squeezed next to each other, pressed against the shelves like people on a mountainside.

"Don't tell him why."

"Well . . ." I was afraid I'd tell him just because it was funny and because—this isn't a good reason—he and I were grown-ups and Leah was a child. I took the canister of sugar and stepped back out without opening the door very wide. I was having trouble not laughing.

"Is anything wrong?" said Gilbert.

"I have to show you something in the living room," I said. "Come on."

"Why? What's wrong?" Gilbert said, but I took him by the arm and led him to the front of the apartment. The living room was the only room Leah wouldn't have to cross to reach her bedroom. I took him all the way to the front of it and pointed to what was out the window, so he'd have his back to her, but I couldn't think of anything to say about the view outside, so I whispered the truth.

"I thought it was a cat," he whispered back.

Elaine would have talked—loudly and with glee—about the house across the street and how a man was trimming a hedge in front of it, but Gilbert was silent. After a minute I heard Leah tiptoe barefoot behind us. Then came the slow squeak of her bedroom door closing, and we went back to the kitchen and drank our coffee, but after a few swallows Gilbert put down his cup and glanced over his shoulder. "Does she do that sort of thing a lot?" he said in a low voice. He sounded critical, though I could tell that he only wanted to sound concerned.

"What sort of thing?"

"Maybe the two of you are alone too much, Amy. The *rivalry* there . . . hiding in the closet."

"No," I said, "she's just modest. It was the nightgown. She must have gone in when Elaine came. Imagine— Elaine used to dress her and change her diapers."

I was sitting opposite him and I ate some strawberries myself. They were sweet. I could make shortcake. My elbows were on the table and so were Gilbert's, and we were both leaning forward a little. I saw that the black still in his hair, with the gray mixed in, looked almost blue, and I thought how we both wear blue a lot and seem to be blue and gray *people*. My ex-husband, John, was different. He was all earth tones—browns and orangey colors. If he were a dog, he'd be one of those liver-colored dogs.

"And I still haven't *seen* Leah," Gilbert said. "After all, it's not as if we have the whole day. And it's not as though there are others. . . ."

He was alluding once more to all those people who didn't exist—the brothers and sisters who had neglected to be born between us, and now also the nieces and nephews they'd have given him. With all of them around, it was true, we two would have been easier together. There would be a brother and two sisters, I decided. I'd be closest to the middle child, Nancy—she'd be fat, with a keen sense of humor, and would fly in periodically from someplace. We'd stay up all night talking—she'd tell hilarious, painful stories of bad jobs, bad men. If she were with us right now, she'd tell closet stories, each funnier than the one before.

"It *is* a shame about this afternoon," I said. "Remember Elaine, the friend you met? I promised to spend it with her. She's having a hard time."

"I'm sure she has a busy schedule, too," said Gilbert edgily. "It *had* to be today." He pushed his chair back from the table a little. "I know you think it was cute—her hiding in the closet. But I think I ought to say it just seemed rude to me."

"Gilbert—" I said, standing up, but then I thought I heard Leah's door open, and I stopped talking and busied myself going for a sponge to clean up some spilled coffee. What came to my mind was something that happened once when I was about four, and our family spent a day at a park. It's the earliest memory I have in which I know someone is mistaken but cannot explain, and it comes back again and again.

Gilbert didn't usually look after me, but on that day he

kept me company while I walked down from the picnic grounds to the lake. There was a stone bridge, and I ran out on it, but it had a wall on either side, taller than I. Gilbert picked me up and sat me on the wall. I don't remember the lake as I saw it from the wall, but I remember his hands gripping my waist as I sat there, my legs stuck straight out in front of me—and I remember my father sprinting down the hill from the picnic grounds, furious with him. "How could you be so *stupid*?" he shouted, while I couldn't say what I knew: that though Gilbert might do me harm in some way, it would never be in *that* way; his hands on my waist were as firm as if they'd grown there, and nothing could make him let go of me.

Now Leah came in, all in blue—jeans and a blue T-shirt—like a member of the family. No doubt our imaginary brothers and sisters would have worn blue, too.

"Hi," she said. She reheated her English muffin in the toaster oven and drank her juice while she waited for it.

"How's school, Leah?" Gilbert said.

"All right. It's over." Leah didn't sit down. She did start to talk, carrying her muffin around, taking bites out of it. She moved back and forth behind Gilbert, then came around and moved back and forth behind me, so one of us had to keep turning to look at her.

"You remind me of someone in a movie," she said to Gilbert. "Not *that* movie," she added, looking at me. "Just any movie."

"Which is '*that* movie'?" he asked her.

"About World War Two," she said. "I was telling Mom."

"I get it," said Gilbert. "Spies, right?"

But Leah paid no attention. "You're my only uncle, did

you know that? An uncle seems like someone in a movie. My father has a sister, but she's not married. I guess you know my father?"

"Of course," said Gilbert. "How is John?" he asked me.

"He's fine," I said.

"He's running around a lot," said Leah. "I don't mean women, I mean work. He has to go on business trips." John was in Texas that week, in fact—otherwise Leah would have been spending the day with him.

"So can I stay home this afternoon, Mom?" she said then, after a moment.

"This afternoon?" I said quickly. "You have a date with Molly for this afternoon."

"I know," said Leah, "but that was so you could be with Elaine. But she sounded all right. I *knew* she'd be fine. And anyway, she canceled. I heard her."

When she said that, Gilbert was turned away from me— she happened to be on his side of the room—facing her. So I couldn't see his face. His hand had been lying lightly on the table, on its side, but now he flattened it onto the tabletop as if he were trying to hold on. I didn't say anything.

"All right?" said Leah.

"We'll talk about it later," I said.

Gilbert stood up. Then he cupped his hand at the edge of the table and carefully swept his strawberry hulls into it, and then he stood holding them for a long time before he asked where he should put them. "I'll do it," I said stupidly, but my eyes indicated the garbage pail and he found it himself.

Gilbert stayed for just a little while longer, but he didn't sit down again. "You people have a busy social life," he said. Then he turned and read a clipping from the newspaper that was taped to my refrigerator. Next he moved to the sink and washed his hand, just the one that had held the hulls, sticking it under the cold water. He stood holding it out as if he were waiting for it to dry. A dish towel hung there, but I didn't point it out.

"Well, Myra sent regards," he said then, speaking of his wife. "Next year she'll try to come along with me." Finally he patted his hand on his pants and moved toward the door. "Next year, maybe we can make a day of it," he said, turning for kisses. "Maybe we can plan a picnic."

THE

LAST

WEDDING

PRESENT

"If I had any brains I'd retire from teaching," said Rosemary, Ronnie's mother. "Then I'd have the energy to make the house bearable." Ronnie was spending a week with her parents, and she'd offered to mop the kitchen floor.

"I'm bearing it," said Ronnie, but her sister, Maddy, was driving in from Oakland for a visit that afternoon and bringing her baby, who would be down on the floor—which was dirty—now that she could crawl. Ronnie filled the bucket and started mopping the dark-red kitchen linoleum under the back window, which looked out toward walnut trees, then made her way to the dining room doorway. Rosemary went off to take a shower. When Ronnie finished mopping, she carried the pail of water through the dining room, around her mother's loom. Ronnie did not spill any water on the living room rug, but what she was doing felt incorrect somehow. She opened the front door and stepped outside to throw away the dirty water, and as she stood there, watching the water she flung spin out in the sun and sink into the ground, feeling cold in her turtleneck and sweater—but not *too* cold (for she was home, outside Modesto, in central California, where winter was distinct but not harsh, not the way it was in the eastern places where she'd been living)—her father, rosy-cheeked, in a heavy sweater, came around the corner of the house. Then Ronnie remembered how her mother used to wash the kitchen floor, at least during the looser, odder time of her youth after her sister and two brothers (all at least nine years older than Ronnie) had left home. In those days her mother always washed the kitchen floor in the evening. Ronnie and her father would be in the living room, her father reading and Ronnie doing homework cross-legged in the big chair. As far as they knew, Rosemary, who was an English teacher at Davis High School, would be correcting papers at the kitchen table, but at some point, once every few weeks, she'd get sick of compositions and would mop the floor instead. She'd begin at the dining room doorway, where Ronnie, just now, had finished, and would mop to the back door. Then she'd let herself out and walk around the house. She'd come to the front door and ring the doorbell, and, inside, Ronnie's father would arrange his face in the curious, courteous expression he wore for his students—he taught anthropology at Modesto Junior College—who sometimes dropped in. Saying over his shoulder, "I didn't hear a car . . . ," he'd open the door and Rosemary would come in laughing. Ronnie thought now that her mother had probably relished that secret walk around the house in the dark. She must have looked into the lighted windows and seen them.

Ronnie had been born a couple of years after her parents and their older children had moved to Modesto from New York, her father escaping from a job at a college in West-chester County where he was misunderstood, or thought to be too radical, or they didn't like Jews, or they got tired of the fact that he never turned in grades on time. When it came time to go, he wrote to one hundred colleges chosen at random from the *Information Please Almanac*, and Modesto Junior College wrote back. In Modesto he and Rosemary discovered they could afford to buy a house on the edge of an old walnut grove. For some reason Leo Goldstein never got into trouble at his new job, though the town was conservative and he was not. Leo's students went hiking with him in Yosemite. In the brief valley winter, he invited them over and made cocoa for them from scratch.

"Do you want to walk out for the mail with me?" Leo said now to Ronnie, who put down her pail and fell into step beside him. It was definitely too early for the mail.

"Are you expecting something?" she said.

"You never know." Ronnie had discovered as she grew up that at other people's houses mail might lie in the box for hours. She herself had inherited her father's feeling that the mail couldn't wait. She'd just gotten a new job (as a legal aid lawyer in New Haven, Connecticut), and when she was waiting to hear whether or not she'd been hired, she assumed there would be a letter and put her anxiety out of her mind each day once the mail had arrived. She was startled when the job offer came over the telephone.

"I like to make sure," said Leo. Maybe it was bad news

he expected. Maybe he liked believing that there is only one window in the day through which anything—bad or good—can fall into one's life from outside. A few years ago, her brother Jonathan's long attack on their father— on his life, his personality, his beliefs—had come by letter, many letters, sometimes more than one a day, then only one every few months, then none. Now Jonathan was courteous but distant. He lived in Spain. But he wrote of coming home for a visit, he described their mother's graying red hair and complained that photographs didn't catch the exact color, and sometimes he suggested a book or a record he thought Leo might like. Jonathan was an actor who earned his living teaching English. "There is nothing wrong with *that*," Leo said now and then, and seemed to mean it, though he had been pleased that Ronnie became a lawyer and Paul, the oldest, a doctor. Maddy had worked in a bookstore until Nicole, the baby, was born.

Leo stuck his hand into the mailbox and felt around. It was too early. "I thought maybe there'd be a letter from your boyfriend," he said.

"I don't have a boyfriend," said Ronnie, as defensively, to her surprise, as she would have ten years earlier.

"Only teasing," said her father. Traffic on the road was heavy, and the noise of passing cars silenced him for a moment. Then, "I thought you were the one who wasn't touchy," he said. He'd said it a hundred times. She didn't answer, but in a moment he went on in a casual, friendly voice. "Didn't Rosemary say you were seeing someone?"

"Oh, that was nothing much," she said.

"A dalliance," said her father, and she laughed.

"Everything's big for your mother," he continued. "The woman lives as if she's in a nineteenth-century novel. Five hundred pages of passion. Mostly imaginary." They had reached the house, and he picked up the pail, which Ronnie had left on the steps. "I hope imaginary," he added. He looked at his watch. "It used to come by now," he said.

•

Maddy was smoking again—it had made her sick when she was pregnant. Now, every time she finished a cigarette, Rosemary emptied the ashtray. The baby didn't quite crawl after all, but peacefully rolled over on her side and played with Rosemary's keys in the middle of the living room rug. Ronnie lay down on her stomach and held the keys up for her niece, jingling them, and Nicole laughed.

"If I were willing to do that all day, my life would be simpler," Maddy said. Rosemary had gone out of the room. She was looking for something, a package she wanted Ronnie to deliver.

"Is it hard, being a mother?" said Ronnie.

"Well, sometimes it's boring," Maddy said. "It's odd— I remember taking care of you and never being bored. I just kept thinking of silly things to do."

"That was nice of you."

"Now I'd rather read."

"This is great, Ronnie," said Rosemary, coming in with a package. "I don't know when I'd have gotten to the post office." The package was a wedding present for a former student of Rosemary's, a favorite, now newly married and living in New Haven, where Ronnie was just about to start work. The package was wrapped in brown paper but not taped. It was a tablecloth and four napkins that Rosemary had woven on her loom, and it was for Gretchen Harris, a gifted girl who wrote poems and who had lingered one day, Rosemary had once told Ronnie, to throw her arms around her teacher's neck and cling to her in tears. When Ronnie was nine or ten, the only child still at home, Gretchen had been her baby-sitter.

"I met Gretchen's mother in the market," Rosemary said now, "and I knew I knew her, but I couldn't figure out who she was. But I pretended I did, because she knew me."

"You would," said Maddy.

"Finally she said the name Gretchen." Rosemary drifted to the window and looked out. Her wavy hair was the way Ronnie had always known it, pulled back into a wide barrette. She was wearing a green sweater and a denim skirt. Outside, it was starting to get dark. "She told me Gretchen was marrying someone at Yale, a scientist," said Rosemary. "Gretchen herself is a physiotherapist, I think. She didn't go on with her English." She sat down and opened one flap of the brown paper parcel. "I have to show you girls this." She pulled out a gift-wrapped package and loosened the Scotch tape. The tablecloth and napkins were brilliant blue and maroon. Rosemary unfolded the tablecloth. "I loved that girl," she said.

The present was extraordinary. Maddy took one of the napkins and carried it to the window. "You know, Mom," she said, holding the napkin spread over her hand, her cigarette well out of the way, "you've outdone yourself."

Rosemary started to fold the tablecloth again, but then Nicole began to cry. Maddy put down the napkin, stubbed out her cigarette, and crossed the room. Her face and Rosemary's were turned the same way, toward Nicole and also Ronnie, and when Ronnie was in New Haven later that winter, walking home from work in the snow—she'd equipped herself with a bright turquoise parka and water-

proof boots—she found that she often pictured her mother
and sister that way, both faces held at an alert tilt, both
women's hands out.

.

Gretchen seemed delighted when—many weeks later,
though it was still winter in Connecticut—Ronnie phoned
on a Sunday morning and asked to deliver the present. She
said she'd heard that Ronnie lived in New Haven now and
had been meaning to look her up. "We have a couple of
friends coming over, but that's *fine*," she said.

"Oh, I won't stay," said Ronnie. Foster Street, where
Gretchen and her husband lived, was a good distance for
a walk, which was just what Ronnie wanted that morning.
She hung up, and then she rewrapped the present, which
had been sitting on the bookcase all this time. It didn't
have the brown paper around it—Rosemary had just re-
packed it in the gift wrap—and Ronnie's cat, a gray tiger
kitten she'd adopted the week after she started her new
job (a son of her managing attorney's cat) had taken to
sleeping on the package and had torn the paper. Ronnie
had finally remembered to buy a package of gift wrap, and
now she sat cross-legged on her bed with tape and scissors,
doing it nicely, and suddenly (she planned her whole day
as she worked) full of energy. She'd been lonely and a
little down. Outdoors it was cold but sunny, and by the
time she rang the doorbell on Foster Street she knew her
cheeks were red. Her hands and feet tingled as she stepped
inside, smelling bacon, and found herself in a cluster of
people, drinks and plates in their hands, in the wide central
foyer of Gretchen and her husband's apartment. It wasn't

a couple of friends, but a party: a brunch, Gretchen explained—she said she was Gretchen but Ronnie didn't recognize her—coming forward.

"Let me take your coat. This is awfully nice of you— and of Rosemary." She took the package. Ronnie followed her into the kitchen, but shook her head—she didn't want to hand over the turquoise parka. "It's just some friends," Gretchen said. "Have you eaten?" Ronnie thought irrelevantly that at least she should be carrying a purse—she had simply put her key into her pocket. She refused a plate of food but picked up a cheese danish and began to nibble on it. "Come meet my husband," Gretchen said.

There were three or four people standing and eating in the living room, and they looked at her with expectant smiles. Gretchen's husband was called Michael, and he turned out to be a tall, black-haired man who looked a little like Ronnie's brother Jonathan. His hairline was receding but his hair was combed back off his face as if he didn't mind at all: the large forehead gave him a frank look. Ronnie put out her hand and looked up at him, the sun in her eyes. The room was almost square, clean and simply furnished and drenched in sunlight, which made the gathering seem like—what?—a wedding, Ronnie decided, not sure why, trying to remember if there was a wedding breakfast in a sunny room somewhere in a book. It almost seemed as if Gretchen and Michael's wedding reception had persisted all these months until this last gift finally arrived—because that's how people acted, as happy to see her as if they'd been waiting for her.

"We heard you were on your way," said a man. "We heard you were a determined walker."

"Oh, I'm famous for it," Ronnie said. On the phone, Gretchen had offered to come for the present later, but Ronnie had insisted she felt like a walk.

"Gretchen's been telling us about your mother," said a woman.

"I'm jealous," Michael said. He called to Gretchen, who had gone back to the kitchen, "What's that line you remember her reciting?"

The multitudinous seas incarnadine," Gretchen called out.

"I had a high-school English teacher like that," said a second woman, a small, curly-haired person, all in brown, like a child dressed up as a chipmunk. "She was the greatest love of my life." People laughed, but she wouldn't join in. "No," she said. "I *mean* it."

"What's it like to be the daughter of the incomparable Mrs. Goldstein?" Michael said. "I didn't know there were Goldsteins in Modesto, California."

"My father was from New York originally," Ronnie said. "And Mom's not Jewish. She's Irish. She was born in Rhode Island."

"But you grew up in California?" said the man. "I thought Californians didn't walk. They drive the car to the corner store for the newspaper and all that."

"Oh, if there's something all Californians do," said Ronnie, "my family does the opposite." They looked at her as if they expected her to go on and be clever, and she found she was happy to talk. "My father has always walked miles every day," she said. "He used to make his students walk with him, like a Greek philosopher. And my older brothers. One of my earliest memories is of being carried around San Francisco on my brothers' shoulders, first one brother, then the other. I think Daddy expected me to walk, too, but I was only about three." She was sorry she hadn't accepted a drink. Not having a glass or a plate in her hand made her feel like a child, like someone listened to with delight for now, but soon to be dismissed. Like a child, too, she was dressed differently from the other guests; being in the turquoise parka seemed something like being in a bathrobe and pajamas, about to be sent off to bed but meanwhile acting charming.

"Nice brothers, to carry you," said one of her audience. "Were they much older than you?"

Ronnie didn't answer for a moment because her eye had been caught by what was happening in the kitchen, in partial view through a doorway and behind Michael. Gretchen was opening the present and showing it to another woman. She shook out the tablecloth and held it up.

"Oh—yes," Ronnie said, recollecting herself. "Jonathan's eleven years older and Paul's thirteen years older. I'm not sure they and my sister trusted my parents to raise me right, especially in Modesto, which they considered the ends of the earth. They were transplanted New York kids."

"This is just gorgeous, Ronnie." Gretchen was bringing the tablecloth and napkins into the living room. "I can't believe she made them herself."

Everyone reached out to finger the nubby cloth. "A tablecloth and three napkins," Gretchen said after a moment. "Three—is that a hint? I don't think I want a baby. But maybe it's just so we can have our single friends to dinner—one at a time."

"Aren't there four napkins?" said Ronnie. "There were four."

She must have dropped it when she rewrapped the package. In fact, now she could *see* it. "This is strange," she said, explaining about the cat and the torn paper—it was possible to be amusing about that, too, it turned out. "I can actually picture it on my bed, open a little, sort of like a parachute. I must have seen it there—subliminally, you know—but it just didn't register. I don't know why, Gretchen. Unless I'm jealous of you because you get to keep my mother's weaving. But I'll go back and get it for you."

"Stay," Michael said. "I'll go along with you later. I'll drive you."

.

She didn't have to wait long, and then they walked after all. "I need a break," said Michael. "If you don't mind." She didn't. He explained to her who all the people at the party were, almost as if he'd known her for a long time and only just met them. "Did you like that brunch?" he said. He didn't wait for an answer. "I didn't. But I liked hearing about your family." Michael said he was also the baby in his family, but he had just one sister. He, too, had grown up feeling looked after. "When I'm working," he said, "and there's something I can't quite get, I sometimes find myself thinking that Sandy would understand it—though in fact she doesn't know science at all. I think it just for a second."

They reached her house and she led him up to her apartment, which was on the third floor. There was no napkin on Ronnie's bed, so she looked under it, and then moved the bed away from the wall to check behind it. Then she looked into the wastebasket, where she'd thrown the old wrapping. She even took out the suitcase she'd used on her trip, and only then did it occur to her that Rosemary might never have put the fourth napkin—the one Maddy carried to the window—back into the package at all. Everything else had been together there on the chair. Ronnie sat down on her bed. "My mother—" she began, and stopped. Michael, all this time, was sitting on a chair opposite her, still in his coat. He'd opened it. He didn't look so much like Jonathan now. He looked happy and excited, and suddenly Ronnie thought he was going to kiss her. She wasn't shocked at the thought—she knew everyone had such thoughts at times. He asked to use the bathroom and she stood up while he was gone and looked out the window at the branches of trees. When he came out, he left. Of course he didn't kiss her—but Ronnie knew that if they met again he might, and they did meet two weeks later at the grocery store. He walked her home and came up for tea, and from then on they were lovers.

"May I come over?" Michael would say on the phone. Ronnie would say yes, because there was no harm in drinking tea with him and explaining why they mustn't sleep together anymore, but once he was there, she didn't explain after all. Ronnie had a single bed, and making love in it was almost comical. Michael was tall, and his arms and legs were too long, and then, too, if they lingered, the cat would join them, walking across their shoulders and purring, butting his head against Ronnie's face. Michael would lift him under his belly and lower him to the floor.

"I keep trying to explain to him," Ronnie would say. "It's not as if you were another *cat*."

"I wish I were," Michael said once, on a cold Sunday afternoon when Ronnie kept trying to cover him with her inadequate blankets. He seemed depressed that day, and now he ran his hand over her entire body—her hair, her face and neck, her breasts and belly and back, down first one leg and then the other. By the end of it they were both laughing and the covers had fallen off.

"At home it's hot by now," Ronnie said, reaching for the blanket. It was April.

He was putting on his shirt. "When I was in Modesto, all I saw were shopping centers."

"There are canals through town," Ronnie said. "You can swim in them."

Michael lay down again in his unbuttoned shirt and she made room for him. "Did you have boyfriends there when you were growing up?" he asked.

"Yes, of course."

"Did you sleep with them?"

"Sometimes," she said. "A little." There had been one boy.

Michael looked at her as if he were going to take her in his arms again, but sat up. "This is crazy," he said.

"I know." But they knew each other's week by now—when the possible times were—and it was easy to make it happen.

Ronnie didn't tell Rosemary and Leo about Michael. She told them on the phone about the missing napkin, and Rosemary said she'd been meaning to mention it. Of course she had it. She'd send it. She'd meant to. In their weekly conversations Rosemary would ask about Ronnie's job and Ronnie would tell her about the cases she'd worked on recently—evictions, landlord-tenant disputes, unemployment cases—and then move on to the more general troubles of her clients, which were many, and to stories of her own confusion when she'd filed a paper late or when, during an unemployment hearing, the referee had scolded her for being too thorough. "Counsel," he'd said, "you won't convince me by reading me the phone book." Now she was taking some time off to study for the bar exam. "It's all hard," she said, and almost talked about Michael.

Once he had said to her, "I was thinking about other women before my wedding."

"You were?" They were eating grilled cheese sandwiches at a luncheonette they'd discovered in West Haven, where they were certain nobody they knew ever came. "Why did you marry her, then?"

"I thought all men had thoughts like that."

"Maybe they do."

"Maybe so. I thought Gretchen was wonderful, don't get me wrong," he said. "Before I even talked to her, I used to look at her earrings. She had tiny earrings shaped like flowers, and I wanted to touch them." They'd met in the cafeteria of a hospital in Washington, D.C., where they'd both worked before Michael had come to Yale. "I decided too fast about her," he said.

.

"But what does Leo Goldstein think?" said Jonathan— as if their father were a book, Ronnie thought.

"We haven't discussed it with him," said Maddy. The question was whether she and her husband, Bruce, should have another child. Nicole was starting to talk now—it was a year since Ronnie's last visit to California.

"I think Leo would like six or seven grandchildren," Jonathan said thoughtfully. "He could conduct little seminars for them."

"I can see it," said Bruce.

The four of them—Jonathan and Ronnie, Maddy and Bruce—were having dinner in a restaurant in San Francisco, where Jonathan had just arrived, coming from Spain via New York. He was going to spend ten days with his parents. Ronnie, who had passed the bar exam and was owed a few days of vacation, had made a plane reservation as soon as she heard Jonathan was coming. Their visits would overlap by two days. She'd been with Leo and Rosemary for three days already, walking, reading, keeping to herself. It was good to be certain Michael wouldn't call her. His calls had become rare, but so necessary to her that she ordinarily could not bear to be away from the phone lest she miss one.

Ronnie had driven to the airport alone in her mother's station wagon to pick up Jonathan. Then Maddy and Bruce had met them in the city. Now the waiter brought their dinners just as Maddy was taking out snapshots of Nicole. Jonathan looked at them slowly, letting his food get cold. "I want kids," he said.

"That's a switch," said Maddy.

"I'm so old," Jonathan said. He was thirty-eight. "People are *grandparents*. . . ." He was living with a woman now, an expatriate American like him. She wasn't sure about children, but Jonathan wanted to marry her and start a family.

"How come you never wanted kids before?" Ronnie said.

"Probably because my parents had kids," said Jonathan. "Now I think it wouldn't be so terrible to be like Leo." He sounded like their father, Ronnie noticed.

"None of us was in a hurry," said Maddy. "Even Paul."

Paul had two children now, but he was well into his thirties before they were born.

"I'm in a hurry," Ronnie said. "I wish I had a baby this minute." She was surprised to hear what she'd said.

"Now why is she different?" Jonathan said. "Same parents as the rest of us. More so, in a way—older. Less diluted by youthful deviations from their true peculiarities." He turned to Bruce. "We always figure out our parents when we get together. It must be boring for you. I suppose you have parents yourself, after all. I guess I even remember them from your wedding. Shall we figure them out?"

"Bruce has parents," said Maddy, "but they're like nice neighbors. They're easy—like, last week was his mother's birthday. I bought her a present I wanted her to like, she liked it, and that was that. But *Rosemary's* birthday . . . I buy her a present I want her to *dislike* . . . I don't send it to her because I can't bear to make her unhappy. Finally I drive out and bring it because I'm mad at her, and she loves it, and I'm overjoyed."

They were all nodding their heads. "I only smoke in my parents' house," said Maddy.

.

When Jonathan's plane came in Ronnie had suddenly been afraid she wouldn't recognize him. She hadn't seen him in four years. The passengers crowded down the corridor from the plane, and then she spotted Jonathan's right cheek—thin, grayish—between the heads of two strangers. He was wearing a dark, zipped-up jacket. His black hair had gray in it. He seemed sad until he saw her.

"So how's your life, Ron?" he said now. They were on their way to Modesto. It was late, and they still had an hour's drive ahead of them. She'd let Jonathan drive.

"I guess it's all right," she said. "My job is hard."

"There's a guy," said Jonathan.

"How do you know?"

"I *don't* know. I'm asking. Is there?"

She stretched her legs out in front of her and braced them on the floor of the car. "I'm in love with a married man named Michael," she said. "I've been sleeping with him for months. He loves me, but he'll never leave his wife." She laughed a little.

Jonathan said, "I'm glad you told me." There was a silence. Then he asked, "How did you meet him?"

"At a party," said Ronnie. "A brunch." She stopped. It wasn't the question she'd wanted and she didn't want to tell Jonathan who Michael was. Jonathan might even remember Gretchen Harris. He'd turn out to have dated her sister or something.

"You go to brunches?" said Jonathan. "I've never been to a brunch."

"No, I don't *go* to *brunches*," Ronnie said. "I just happened to be there. He walked me home—but that was the easy part. Now it's awful. I keep making up my mind to get over him, but I don't."

"How come he walked you home? Wasn't his wife there?"

"Jon," said Ronnie, "you're making me feel bad."

"Oh, God, Ronnie—I'm sorry. I'm really sorry. I was just so curious. I never know how people get started—how they take opportunities. I have to see a woman fifty times before I can start something."

"Nobody sees anybody fifty times."

"I met Sheila because she teaches in the same school I do. I saw her every day."

"Tell me about her," said Ronnie, and for the rest of the drive they talked about Jonathan's life in Spain.

•

The next morning Ronnie drove her mother to work so she and Jonathan could use the station wagon if they needed it. A friend would drive Rosemary home, she said. Jonathan slept all day; after lunch, Ronnie drove to a shopping center and tried to call Michael at his lab from a public phone. He wasn't there but they expected him. She circled the shopping center on foot, took herself slowly through a department store, wishing she'd see something she wanted to buy, and tried again. He was still out, and the same man answered the phone. She couldn't try still another time. When she got home, her parents and Jonathan were in the living room talking. Her mother had just come home from work, and she still had her worn leather briefcase on her lap. Ronnie joined them, and they talked for the rest of the day.

The next day was Ronnie's last in California, a Saturday. She had breakfast with Leo—yogurt and granola. Rosemary and Jonathan were still asleep.

"What's the feeling in legal services these days about class action lawsuits?" said Leo, sprinkling the granola on his yogurt. Then he reached for the jar of raisins.

"I'm not sure," Ronnie began.

But Jonathan came in as she began to explain. "Don't stop," he said. "What?"

"I'm not sure."

"About what?"

"Class action lawsuits." She had started to talk about a suit her office had brought some years ago, but now she didn't feel like explaining. She didn't know much about it.

Jonathan made himself a peanut butter and jelly sandwich. He ate standing up, one hand resting on the windowsill behind the table. Outside, it was raining. The trees looked dark and interesting in the rain, and there was new green grass, though it was early December. "I have to go shopping," Jonathan said. "I don't have anything warm—I should buy a sweater."

"It would give me pleasure to buy you one, Jon," said Leo.

"That's not necessary, Dad. I'd just like to borrow the car."

"I didn't say it would fulfill a need. I said it would give pleasure. Pleasure to me."

"So you did," said Jonathan. "All right, Leo Goldstein, you can buy me a sweater. Thanks. We'll go shopping together. You can tell me about your teaching and so forth. I'll buy you a cup of coffee."

Leo was still preparing his breakfast, Ronnie noted. After sprinkling raisins on his yogurt, he'd carefully peeled an apple and sliced it into the bowl.

"Look," he said to her, as gently as if she were a child, "the peel came off in one piece." When she was small, Ronnie remembered, her mother would try to peel apples for pie that way. When there was a long strip of peel, Ronnie would throw it over her shoulder. The letter of the alphabet it formed would be the initial of the man she'd marry. Now, on her way to the sink with her empty bowl, she shrugged, glanced at Jonathan, tossed the peel over her shoulder, and turned to look at it.

"*M*," said Jonathan. He'd been paying attention then, driving home the other night. She was pretty sure she'd said Michael's name only once.

"No, it's a *W*," she said. "William. Opposing counsel in my big case—that'll be funny, marrying *him*."

.

It rained steadily all morning. Rosemary washed her hair and wrapped it in a towel. She was trying to straighten her workroom, the room she used now for preparing classes, marking papers, and sewing. It had been Jonathan's, and he was sleeping there on this visit. Jonathan and Leo had gone shopping right after breakfast.

"I should have cleaned it up last week," Rosemary said to Ronnie, who'd come in to watch her. Rosemary's hair was wrapped in a green towel, and she was wearing a blue quilted bathrobe. Ronnie was restless. She had carried in a cup of coffee and was sitting on the bed. After a while she spotted a bit of color under a pile of the papers her mother was looking over. "What's that?" she said, and leaned over to reach for it.

"Oh, you know what that is?" said Rosemary. "It's the napkin I never sent to Gretchen Harris. That's really appalling."

"You're impossible," said Ronnie. "I assumed you sent it months ago."

"Yes, anybody else would have," her mother said. "But do you ever see those people? I don't suppose I can ask you to deliver it *again*?"

Ronnie laughed. She picked up the napkin, which was

a little soiled but would wash. She could give it to Michael—it would be an excuse to see him—but what would he say to Gretchen? They'd figure out something. "All right," she said.

She drank her coffee and fingered the fabric. "I was hoping you'd make friends with them," Rosemary said. "Were they nice people? Did Gretchen remember me?" She looked wistful, and Ronnie thought of the welcome she'd had at the brunch, and the woman in brown who loved her English teacher better than anyone.

"Oh!" she said. "I never told you! I called her up—it was a Sunday morning, and I felt like taking a walk. And she said sure, come ahead—but when I got there it was a brunch, and she'd been telling the guests all about you."

"About me?"

"Yes. She *reveres* you." Ronnie laughed again. Rosemary looked so perplexed and pretty, pulling off the towel and raking her fingers through her gray-streaked longish hair, that Ronnie wanted only to convey to her what it had been like: how Gretchen carried in the tablecloth to show her friends, even how Michael said he was jealous of Rosemary. Ronnie was so eager, her words came out so fast, it was as if she were telling the whole story. She told about the woman in brown and how she wouldn't join in the laughter.

"And this poor young couple has been waiting for the fourth napkin all this time," said Rosemary. "She sent me a lovely note, but it wasn't personal. She never mentioned the missing one."

Ronnie had rolled the square of fabric on her knee, and now she unrolled it and folded it into fourths. Her mother was sorting the papers and throwing some into the wastebasket next to her desk. "I remember lots of kids I've taught," she said. "But I never think they'll remember me."

"Well, that one did," Ronnie said.

Rosemary stopped sorting papers now and moved to a pile of clothes on a chair. "These need mending," she said. "This would be a good day for it." She picked up a pair of pants and looked them over. Her sewing box was on top of Jonathan's old dresser. She walked over and put her hand on it, but then turned to Ronnie as if she'd been thinking something for a while.

"Do you love anybody right now, baby?" she said.

"No," said Ronnie quickly, alarmed.

But Rosemary, her hand still on the sewing box, her other hand fingering the quilted satin of her robe, turned to Ronnie. "*I* do, actually," she said. "I'm in love with someone."

"You don't mean Daddy?" Ronnie blurted out.

"No," said Rosemary with a little laugh. "I don't mean Daddy. Though I love him too." She opened the sewing box and took out a spool of thread. Then she searched for a needle. "I didn't mean to shock you," she said. "I thought you might have guessed."

"No," said Ronnie. "How would I guess?"

"I don't know." She gave up looking and sat down again with the thread in one hand and the pants in the other. "Find me a needle, would you, sweetie?" she said. Ronnie began to sift through the sewing basket. There were a few loose needles at the bottom. She threaded one for her mother, who wasn't wearing her reading glasses.

"His name is James," said Rosemary. "He's the father of a student. He's divorced. Younger than I am."

"Dad doesn't know?" said Ronnie.

"He knows I'm susceptible to outbreaks of the disease," Rosemary said. "This is the first time in ages it's gone this far. I love your father, heaven knows—but in a way he's like a little *elf*." She began sewing up the open seam in the pants, frowning because she wasn't wearing her reading glasses. "When I go to the market," she said, "I think I might meet James. Once, I did. How do people do the shopping if there isn't someone like that?"

Ronnie laughed a little, but she remembered meeting Michael in the grocery store in New Haven and how she had looked for him every time after that. She wasn't glad that she did what Rosemary did; it seemed, clearly, *not* like the way she wanted to buy her groceries.

"What worries me is that Jonathan will find out," Rosemary went on. "If Jonathan knows, everyone will know."

"What do you mean?"

"He can't help it," Rosemary said. "Haven't you ever noticed that about him? Everything's just so *interesting* to him. And he'll probably simply guess it—he's like that, you know, especially about sex. When he was a little kid, any time Leo and I sneaked into our bedroom during the day, he'd sense it, wherever he was. He could be playing half a mile away, but as soon as we had our clothes off, he'd be knocking at our door. 'Mom, I hurt my knee.' "

Ronnie shook her head. She felt anxious. She hadn't been out all day. She'd had too much coffee. Maybe she should go for a walk, rain or no rain.

"And as soon as he guesses, he'll tell Leo," Rosemary said. "He'll be here another week. He'll have to find *something* awful to tell Leo during that week."

Outside, there was the sound of a car in the driveway,

the complaining sound a car makes in the rain. "Here they are," said Rosemary. She went into the living room to open the door, and Ronnie followed her. Jonathan came in smiling, with a bag under his arm and the mail in his hand. Leo was behind him. He was wearing a little cotton hat to keep off the rain. Jonathan's head was bare.

"Hi," said Jonathan. "I have a new sweater."

"Is that the mail?" Rosemary said, stepping forward. "Hi."

Jonathan had balanced the pile of letters and circulars on the back of a chair while he unzipped his jacket. Now he picked up the mail again, but then he waited, the letters in his hand, before he offered them to his mother. Did he actually hold them just out of her reach for a moment? "Are you expecting something, Rosemamma?" It had been his pet name for her years ago. Then, "What's that, Ron?" he said, as he turned to hand Rosemary the stack of letters and looked at Ronnie behind her.

"No, there's nothing for your mother," said Leo.

"What?" said Ronnie, looking where Jonathan was pointing, at her hand. She was still holding Gretchen and Michael's napkin.

"It's beautiful. Did Mom make it?" Jonathan reached for it and Ronnie handed it to him.

"I need to get out," she said. "I don't care about the weather." She went into the room where she was staying, the one she and Maddy had shared, and took her coat from the closet, and tied a scarf over her hair. Then she sat on the bed in her coat for a few moments. She tried to remember exactly what she had said to Jonathan about Michael in the car the other night. Then she went back to the living room. Jonathan and her parents had gone into the kitchen. The napkin was on the chair back where Jonathan had balanced the mail. Ronnie took the napkin and carried it to her father's desk in the corner. In his wastebasket she found a used manila envelope that had brought one of the journals to which he subscribed. She scratched out the address and the return address. Then she put her parents' address in the top left corner and addressed the envelope to Gretchen and Michael in New Haven.

"Dad," she called, "do you have any stamps?" She was already rummaging in his drawer. He came to the kitchen doorway and looked at her over his shoulder, a short man with a crease in his forehead. "I have stamps," he said. There was a book of them. She didn't know how heavy the envelope was. She took eight stamps, to be certain. "Do you need to mail something?" said Leo. "If you put it in our box, it won't be picked up until Monday."

"Can you lend me your car?" she said. "I'll drive it to the post office."

"I'm not sure the post office is open," he said. "Of course you can take the car. But wouldn't you be better off taking the letter with you tomorrow—if you're sending it back east, that is?"

"No, this is better," said Ronnie. "This is fine." She just wanted to see the envelope disappear into a mailbox. She closed the fastener, and then she spotted a roll of tape and taped the flap. She smiled at Leo. He looked worried— worried for her important mail. "I need to buy some things anyway," Ronnie said. Leo reached into his pocket for the car keys. She took them and touched his arm in its old blue sweater. He watched her as she went out. He had a tentative look about him, a listening look.

Ronnie went outside and flung herself into his old, damp, familiar car, a fifteen-year-old Plymouth, and turned on the wipers. The driveway was rutted, and when she drove through puddles, water splashed out sideways in sheets, which pleased her, for some reason.

Ronnie paused at the foot of the driveway to check for traffic, and made the turn. The word *brunch* would do it, she reflected, or any of a dozen other words, probably, and surely, in the next week, one of those words would be spoken in her parents' wordy household, and Jonathan would say, "How about Ronnie and that guy at the brunch?" and when he explained, Rosemary would make the connection. Ronnie didn't mind—she found that she didn't mind after all—as long as she wasn't there. She'd be gone, high in the sky on that plane tomorrow, freer even than she felt now (and she was heady with freedom, driving easily down the road toward town, her manila envelope beside her) or already in New Haven, where, the first week she was home, two different men—nice men—would ask her out for coffee, because new freedom can be detected when a man looks at a woman—or a woman at a man— and everyone wants to get near it.

Alice Mattison runs the Anderson Street Writing Workshops in New Haven, Connecticut, where she lives with her husband and three sons. She is also the author of a novel, *Field of Stars;* a collection of stories, *Great Wits;* and a book of poems, *Animals.*